Into The Red

The Murder Mile Ser

Christine Pattle

Chapter 1

Rose Marsden wanted to cry for the millionth time this week as she dragged her suitcase up the communal staircase to her mother's flat. Three flights seemed to go on forever as her burden became heavier with each step up.

Was it really less than a fortnight ago when her almost perfect life had been destroyed, not once, not twice, but three times? The intense shock of that final blow, losing her mother in such a dreadful way, threatened to stay with her for a long time.

Below her, a door clicked open, followed by a familiar voice rising up the stairwell.

"Rose? Is that you?" Dorothy's voice floated up from outside her flat on the ground floor.

Rose swallowed the lump in her throat. "Yes, it's me. I'm back."

Dorothy pattered slowly up the stairs, stopping to catch her breath before she finally reached Rose. "What happened?"

Rose turned towards her, struggling to hold back the tears.

"Oh, dear, you look dreadful. Why don't I put the kettle on and you can come and tell me all about it?"

Rose nodded. She needed someone to talk to, and Dorothy, a good friend of Rose's late mother, was the only person she knew in the area. "Let me dump this in the flat first." Rose pointed to the suitcase.

"I'll leave the door open," Dorothy said. "Don't be long."

Rose dragged her suitcase up the final few steps. She hoped Dorothy still had some of her emergency supply of gin, although they did leave the bottle somewhat depleted earlier in the week. Rose's life seemed to jump from one emergency to another.

She fished the door key out of her handbag. Thank God for Mum's flat. She'd be totally scuppered without it. Leaving her suitcase in the hallway, she locked up again and paused for a few moments to get her breath back before walking down the stairs to Dorothy's flat.

"Hello," she called out as she pushed the open door.

"Come in, dear."

Rose followed the voice into the kitchen. To her relief, a new gin bottle and two glasses graced the middle of Dorothy's table. A steaming hot cup of tea sat next to them. Rose pulled out a chair.

"Do you want to tell me what happened, or shall we drink our tea first? I've got chocolate biscuits." She opened a cupboard and pulled out a packet of biscuits. "Did you patch things up with Philip?"

Rose burst into tears. Dorothy got up and put her arm around her. "There, there. After all you've been through recently, it surely can't be worse than that."

Rose blew her nose before a fresh flood of tears erupted. Was it worse? In the last two weeks, she discovered Philip, her husband, was having an affair, she'd been fired from her job, and then, to top it all off, her mother had been murdered.

Dorothy pushed the box of tissues towards her. Rose pulled one out and dabbed at her eyes. No. She supposed losing her house didn't compare with all that, but it certainly came close.

"Perhaps you should start by telling me why you came back." Dorothy reached for the gin bottle and poured some for Rose, topping it up with a rather too generous amount of tonic. "This morning, you seemed so keen to go home to Manchester and see that husband of yours, so something must have happened."

Was it only this morning when Rose left Brackford to go home to Manchester? It seemed like a lifetime ago. "That husband of mine happened," Rose said bitterly. "When I got home, our house was up for sale and the locks had been changed." She took a large gulp of gin, hoping it would help get her through recounting the agonising events of the day. "It turns out he's been gambling. The bastard gambled away our house." She drained her glass and grasped the gin bottle with both hands, anxious that she might be shaking too much to be able to pour it without spilling any.

"How awful." The shock showed on Dorothy's face, which seemed to have become even more lined and grey in the couple of weeks since Rose first met her after her mother's murder. "How long has that been going on?"

Rose shook her head sadly. "Quite a while, I expect." How did she not notice? Because she didn't want to, that's why. Small signs, but obvious ones: a lack of money in their joint account well before the end of every month, and her bank card got declined only a few days ago. But the truth of it proved to be far worse than that. Philip had massacred their joint savings account, then he'd stopped paying the mortgage to give himself more gambling money.

Dorothy patted her hand. "I'm sure your husband was an expert at hiding the evidence. Addicts always are."

Rose struggled to stop herself from crying again. Dorothy being so nice made it worse. Yes, Philip hid so many things from her, but she blamed herself for being so stupid. She never bothered looking at their bank statements. Philip always offered to take care of everything, so why should she worry? He even offered to do the accounts for her small jewellery-making business, so she could use the extra time to make more pieces to sell. It made perfect sense. She hated the accounting side of it. Not that she wasn't perfectly capable, but she found it boring, much preferring the artistic side of the business.

"There, there, dear. At least you've got Iris's flat to live in, and it will be lovely to have you here."

Rose dried her eyes. Without her mother's flat, she'd be homeless. She'd been planning to sell it as soon as the probate on Mum's estate came through, but that would take several months.

"Philip's gone to live with his fancy woman." Rose laughed bitterly. "We'll see how long that lasts now that he's run out of money." Sandra Denison, Philip's mistress, used to be Rose's boss until a couple of weeks ago. The betrayal, by both of them, still stung.

"My mother used to say, *love flies out the window when the bailiffs walk in the door*. It's very true," Dorothy said.

Rose forced a smile. It would serve Philip right if Sandra kicked him out. Rose certainly didn't intend to take him back, not when he'd lost all their money and shacked up with a much younger woman. After twenty-one years, their marriage was well and truly over, and what did she have to show for it? Twenty-one years of worry lines, and now, not a penny to her name. Philip had melted away their assets faster than a tub of ice cream in a blast furnace.

"So where does that leave you?" Dorothy asked.

Rose had been asking herself the same question for the last few hours. "Penniless, jobless, and husbandless." She clenched her fists and breathed in and out deeply, trying to stem the next outpouring of tears. The reality was worse than that. The paltry twenty pounds left in her purse would make no dent in paying off her almost maxed-out credit card, and she'd lost most of her personal possessions. The bailiffs had ransacked the house. Philip threw a few of her clothes into a suitcase and left them with a neighbour. He didn't even have the decency to deliver them to her himself. Instead, he made her collect them from the neighbour. She would never forgive him for the feeling of shame as she knocked at their door and asked for her clothes. The bailiffs took everything else, even her expensive jewellery-making supplies and equipment. How would she ever afford to replace all that?

"I'm sure you'll soon find another job," Dorothy said, trying to be cheerful. "And you can go to the job centre tomorrow to sign on for benefits in the meantime. We'll soon get you sorted out."

The job centre. That would be another walk of shame. How did it come to this? Rose thought she'd long ago escaped her childhood poverty, but it seemed to be coming back to bite her harder than ever.

Dorothy must have noticed Rose staring at the rapidly emptying gin bottle because she poured her another glass without asking, sensibly putting in even less gin and more tonic this time. "Will you be all right with Jordan Taylor still awaiting trial?" Dorothy asked.

Rose shuddered. Since the shock of this afternoon's revelations, she hadn't given Jordan Taylor a second thought. She glanced over at the door as if Taylor might come bursting through it at any moment. The hand holding the glass of gin began to shake. She put the glass on the table and clasped her hands together on her knees before Dorothy noticed. "I'll have to be," she said, bravely forcing a smile. Even with Taylor in police custody and on remand until the trial, Rose still worried that he might get to her through his friends.

"I thought you'd be safe in Manchester," Dorothy said. "It came as a surprise, seeing you back here so soon."

Rose assumed the same thing only this morning, which now seemed like a million years ago. Jordan Taylor murdered her mother only a couple of weeks ago. He confessed as much to Rose, and she'd been lucky to escape being his next victim. Perhaps coming back here wasn't such a good idea after all, but what other choice did she have?

"I'll be happier once he's convicted," she said. The police refused to guarantee that would happen. Taylor still insisted on pleading 'not guilty.'

"I'm sure you'll be ok." Dorothy picked up the gin bottle, now empty, and put it on the draining board. "We'll all look out for you."

"Thank you."

Dorothy's paper-thin skin, stretched across her bony hands, brought home to Rose how little she could rely on a frail lady in her late seventies to look out for her, but she appreciated the sentiment. She resolved to call Detective Constable Farrier tomorrow morning. If Farrier found out she'd returned to the area, perhaps he would keep an eye on her. That thought didn't fill her with confidence, either.

Back in Mum's flat, Rose set about unpacking. However depressing this whole fiasco became, she would have to make the best of it and get on with her life somehow. She laid her sparse collection of clothes on the bed, while she made some room to hang them in Mum's wardrobe.

At least she still had Jack, her and Philip's son. With Jack being at university in Colchester, possibly the only advantage to leaving Manchester was being much closer to him, Brackford being only an hour from Colchester by train. She would love to visit, if having his mum hanging around for an occasional weekend wouldn't cramp Jack's style. She longed to see him. If only he were here now. With a jolt, she remembered she still needed to tell him about her and Philip splitting up and moving house. The news would come as a massive shock to Jack. She would have to confess about the bank repossessing the house, too, otherwise it would be a massive blow if he decided to make an impromptu visit home. She must tell him soon. It's just that every time she tried to put it into words, she burst into tears.

She took her phone out of her bag, wondering how long she would be able to keep up the monthly payments on that. Impulsively, she tapped on Jack's name.

It went straight to voicemail and Rose wondered if he'd seen her name flash up on his phone and rejected the call deliberately. A sickening feeling weighed on her stomach. She would text him tomorrow and suggest visiting him at the weekend. She didn't want to break the news to Jack over the phone that his parents would be divorcing and the family home was gone. By tomorrow, she might have worked out how to pay for the train fare to visit him.

She forced her thoughts back to the here and now. At least she wasn't homeless: her only piece of luck. If this happened a few months later and she'd already sold the flat, Philip would have squandered the proceeds on the horses, or bought thousands of lottery tickets, or any number of the zillion different ways he knew to lose their money, no doubt under the illusion that one day he would get that big win and pay it all back.

Anyway, a two-bedroom flat in dire need of modernisation, in a run-down area of north-east London, hardly qualified as a prime piece of property. And being on the third floor, with no elevator in the block, didn't add to its appeal. The steep stairs seemed to go on forever. How did Mum ever cope with those endless stairs? Rose would be cursing them every time she did a food shop, unless she got it delivered. Except she couldn't afford an extra fiver for delivery. That luxury belonged to her past life. Reality kicked in violently. Not only had she lost her home, her husband, and her friends, she had no money coming in. Nothing, zero, zilch, except for a twenty-quid note in her purse. Barely enough to buy food for a couple of days. She needed to find a job fast.

She wandered into the kitchen and switched on the light. The flicker of the old fluorescent tube in the ceiling reassured her. Quickly, she switched it off, conscious that she mustn't risk clocking up a big electricity bill. A tiny bit of daylight still filtered in through the kitchen window.

A cursory search of the cupboards revealed half a box of tea bags, tins of baked beans, plum tomatoes, and cling peaches, and an unopened packet of pasta. What a relief that she didn't throw everything out this morning.

Rose wondered how much the flat might be worth. Judging by the state of the kitchen, Mum hadn't spent any money on it in years. The whole flat needed a complete refit, as well as redecorating. Woodchip wallpaper gave the flat a cheaper and nastier appearance than it deserved. The flat needed at least ten grand spent on it. Ten might not cover it. Not that it mattered. She didn't even have a spare ten quid at the moment, let alone ten thousand.

The flat's only plus point was its two bedrooms. She hoped Jack would stay with her during the holidays. It would be a huge comedown from the house in Manchester, but the alternative would be staying with his dad and Sandra. Would Sandra welcome Jack? Did she even possess a spare room for him to stay in?

She went into the bathroom. The stark lighting made for a very unflattering picture in the mirror. Her red eyes and tear-stained face didn't help. She splashed some water on her face, then searched for a hairbrush. The tangles gained since this morning closely resembled a bird's nest. The neatly shaped lines of her current hairstyle were already growing out, reminding her she would have to cancel next week's hairdresser appointment.

Rose sat on the edge of the bath. The repulsive avocado bathroom suite screamed last century. A few minutes ago, she'd been thinking that, if she found a job, she might get a small mortgage to cover the expense of doing the place up. Who was she kidding? She couldn't even afford a haircut.

"One step at a time, Rose," she said to herself. "Start looking for a job tomorrow."

Chapter 2

It suddenly hit Rose that she hadn't eaten since breakfast this morning. She decided to pop out to the convenience store down the road to get milk, bread, and butter. With those few extra provisions, she would get by with the stuff in the kitchen cupboards for a day or two. Tomorrow, she would go to the job centre, then find a cheap supermarket.

Picking up her purse, Rose left the flat, locking the door behind her. On her way down, she counted the stairs.

"Thirty-six, thirty-seven, thirty-eight..." she whispered under her breath. If she had to carry everything up all these stairs, she must remember not to buy anything heavy. The suitcase gave her enough trouble.

A movement behind her made her jump.

"Hi there."

Rose turned to see who the voice belonged to, annoyed as she'd forgotten how many steps she'd counted and she was still only two-thirds of the way down. The petite blond woman looked about Rose's age.

"I saw you go upstairs with a suitcase earlier. How long are you staying?"

"I haven't decided," Rose said, despondent that her entire future now looked too uncertain to answer the woman's simple question. "I'll be living here for a while." She hoped that was true, that it would only be for a while. It was just a stopgap until she got herself sorted. She didn't want to settle here permanently. At the back of her mind, her fear of Jordan Taylor refused to leave her, so she couldn't quite bring herself to admit the truth that she may have to stay here for very much longer than planned.

"I moved in today, too. Looks like we're both newbies." The blond woman smiled at her.

"Yes," Rose said, not wanting to explain anything further about how she came to be here.

"I'm Tan."

"Tan?"

"Short for Tanya."

"Of course. My name's Rose."

"If you need anything, I'm at number 3." Tan pointed to a bright red door behind her. "Lovely to meet you, Rose."

"Yes, you too."

Rose descended the rest of the stairs, glad for a friendly neighbour. It seemed a pleasant enough neighbourhood, but it wasn't Manchester. It completely lacked restaurants, cinemas, or any decent social life within walking distance of the flat, and she didn't own a car—Philip persuaded her to sell her car several months ago and share his instead. She hadn't realised until it was too late that *sharing* meant Philip drove the car to work almost every day, and she got to use it about once in every five blue moons, if she was lucky.

Not that she had any friends in this area to be sociable with—a good thing because her budget would barely stretch to a bag of crisps, let alone a meal in a fancy restaurant. But if, or when, her circumstances improved, Brackford wasn't far, and central London only a short train journey away. She needed to make the best of it here and be grateful to have a roof over her head.

It began to get dark as Rose walked to the Hale Hill Stores, making a mental list in her head of what she needed. She must stick to the bare minimum, bread, milk, butter, even though she craved a chocolate biscuit and a glass of wine. But no way would her precious twenty-pound note last long if she splashed out on luxuries like that. Yesterday, Rose would have called such things *essentials*, not luxuries. She reminded herself that she was probably slightly tipsy from Dorothy's gin and she certainly didn't need any more alcohol today.

The old-fashioned bell tinkled as Rose pushed open the shop door.

Bread, milk, butter. Rose repeated the mantra inside her head, determined not to buy anything more. Somehow, she needed to eke out that twenty pounds for a couple of days until she sorted out something else. Spotting some bread, she made a beeline towards it. The loaves of bread seemed to stare back at her as she gazed at them, whilst trying to do the mental arithmetic in her head to work out which loaf would be the best value buy. Her head span with numbers and she settled on the smallest of the loaves, wanting to spend the least amount of money possible and hoping she would have some income by the time she needed more bread.

"I thought you'd gone back to Manchester."

Startled, Rose turned around quickly, searching among the cluttered shelves for the source of the voice.

Roman Marek, the shop's owner, appeared from behind the till. Rose was pleased to see him. He'd been very friendly and helpful to her over the last few days as she organised her mother's funeral.

"There's been a change of plan." Rose forced a smile, trying to make light of her disastrous day. "I'm going to live in Mum's flat for a while."

"That's nice. Your mum would be pleased."

The events of the day were catching up with Rose, with exhaustion setting in fast. "I need to get going," she said, remembering how much Roman liked to talk once he got started. Over the last few days, he had already recounted most of his life history to her, since he moved here as a young boy from Poland with his parents. "I just need some milk and butter."

"The fridges are right at the back of the shop." He pointed, unnecessarily, as Rose remembered perfectly well.

Rose grabbed her tiny loaf of bread and hurried to the end of the aisle. With a bit of luck, another customer would come in soon, then she would pay for her purchases and leave before Roman started talking for hours. Much as she liked him, after her dreadful day, she simply wanted to get home and relax with a nice cup of tea. She searched the fridge for milk but only found two-pint bottles. That would eat further into her twenty pounds, but she supposed it would be more cost-effective in the long run to buy a larger quantity. She grabbed a bottle and searched for some butter.

The doorbell tinkled as another customer entered. Rose smiled with relief. That would make it much easier to pay for her items and leave quickly.

"What do you want?" At the other end of the shop, Roman's voice sounded agitated.

Whatever was happening, Rose decided to wait here for another minute.

"We want our money." The voice, with the implied threat behind it, made Rose shudder. After her recent experience of being attacked by her mother's murderer, she became nervous around any potential violence. She strained to listen, unable to see what was going on from the far corner of the shop. Best to stay here until they left. Best not to get involved. She held her breath and crouched down, cowering in the corner, desperate to avoid any confrontation.

"I don't have the money." Roman's voice came out in barely a whisper, but it carried through the silence.

You and me both, Rose thought, picking up on the desperation in his voice and wishing she could help him.

A man laughed. "Then you'll have to pay another way." A different voice, deeper and raspier. A crashing noise that sounded like cans and jars falling on the floor resounded round the shop.

"I can get you the money," Roman said. "Please stop. I'll get you the money tomorrow. Please, you can't do that." His voice reeked of despair.

"We can do what we like," the first man said.

More noises followed, the dull thud of cardboard boxes hitting the floor. Rose's body froze. Did these men intend to trash the entire shop? How long would it be before they discovered her hiding place? She looked for a way out. The only exit was through the front door. There was no chance of her making a run for it without being seen.

A big mirror hung near the ceiling above Rose. She didn't notice it before but guessed it would be strategically angled to spot shoplifters from the other end of the shop. Worried she might be visible from where the men stood, she shrunk back against the shelves, praying the men wouldn't glance this way and see her reflection. Near the edge of the mirror, she saw something of the events unfolding at the other end of the shop. But although it gave her a good view of Roman, the two unknown men remained out of range.

The clatter of metal and glass jangled Rose's already taut nerves. She realised she was shaking.

"Please stop. I can get you the money. You must stop this," Roman begged.

Rose watched Roman's reflection in the mirror powerlessly as he ran forwards. A beefy-looking man came partially into view as he lunged at Roman, but Rose only saw a brief glimpse of the man's back, then he moved out of range. For a second, Roman seemed to freeze in mid-air before collapsing heavily to the floor.

"Oh my God, what have you done?"

Rose wasn't sure which of the men the voice belonged to. Roman gave a loud groan. The edge of the beefy man's black leather jacket moved back into view, motionless in front of Roman's prone body.

"Shut up, Terry."

Rose tried to shift position quietly so she might see more than the man's sleeve, but it made no difference.

"But he needs help."

The speaker's voice wavered. He sounded younger, and his tone was less hard than beefy man. Rose assumed the younger-sounding man must be Terry. Perhaps Terry would use beefy man's name.

"I said, shut up, Terry. We need to get out of here. Now," the beefy man spoke again. "Come on, before anyone shows up."

Terry moved towards Roman, where he lay on the floor. Rose only saw the top of his baseball cap, a nondescript navy blue, and the sleeve of his black jacket. Not even the colour of his hair showed. The police would inevitably ask her for a description, but that was the least of her worries right now. She just wanted the men to go. If they found her now... she didn't want to think about what might happen to her.

Suddenly, the beefy man grabbed the arm of the other man, Terry, dragging him towards the door.

Rose held her breath, scared she might cry or sneeze, or make some other sound that would give away her hiding place. The doorbell signalled the door opening, then she heard it swing shut. For several seconds, silence descended on the shop. Rose peeped apprehensively around the corner of the shelving to check the men had really gone. She would wait a few seconds to make sure. Silently, she counted up to ten. ...*eight, nine, ten*. She forced herself to get up, her legs wobbling as she walked the first few steps, fearing they might collapse underneath her, terrified of what she would find.

Chapter 3

As Rose moved along the far aisle of the shop, stepping carefully over the debris of broken glass and dented tins, the extent of the damage shocked her. She ran the last few steps, her body finally responding to the urgency of the situation.

"Roman. Mr Marek. Can you hear me?" The shopkeeper lay sprawled on the floor, face down. Rose knelt next to him and turned him over, straining with the weight of him. The sight of blood oozing from his stomach made her jolt momentarily backwards in shock. She glanced around for something to stop the bleeding but saw nothing suitable. Quickly, she removed her coat. She'd come out in a hurry, throwing her coat on over her T-shirt, intending to be home again within a few minutes. Without hesitation, she pulled off the T-shirt, folded it up, and pressed it hard against the wound.

"You're going to be ok, Roman. Don't worry."

Her body worked on automatic pilot, despite the overwhelming numbness that enveloped her. She found her phone and dialled the emergency services. "Ambulance and police. It's urgent. Someone's been stabbed." Rose didn't remember the shop's name or address, so she gave Mum's address, with directions from there. A five-minute walk. They could drive the distance in a few seconds.

The wound didn't look good. Roman's attacker must have taken the knife with him. Rose had watched enough TV, hundreds of crime dramas that Phillip made her sit through over the years, to realise that removing the knife was a really bad thing to do. If only they left the knife in the wound, it would plug the hole and stop much of the bleeding. She pressed on the T-shirt as hard as she could. She'd purchased the T-shirt a few years ago when she and Philip had gone to the Indie Rock Festival near Manchester. To her horror, her hasty arrangement of the T-shirt had resulted in the word *indie* being folded in half, leaving the word *DIE* staring her in the face. She looked away, trying to ignore it, but her eyes kept getting drawn back to the word. It had better not be a bad omen.

Despite her efforts to stem the flow, Roman's blood covered her hands and the lower half of her jeans where she knelt on the floor. It didn't matter. The only thing that mattered was to stop this man from dying.

"Can you hear me?" Rose asked again, staring at his face as if that might make him spring to his feet. "Roman, speak to me. It's going to be all right. The ambulance is on its way." Roman didn't answer. She knew that was a bad sign. Where were the paramedics? She needed them here, now.

She took Roman's wrist in one hand, trying to detect a pulse. It felt faint, so faint that she wondered if her imagination had conjured it up. She kept pressing on the wound. He was such a nice man, and so friendly and welcoming to her when she first came to this area after her mother's death a couple of weeks ago. He didn't deserve this. She felt guilty that only a short time before, she'd wanted to hurry home and make a cup of tea. Tea wouldn't be much use to her now. She needed a stiff drink.

Rose checked her watch again. How long would it take the ambulance to get here? Surely, they should be here by now.

Roman's wife, Sarah, and their two daughters lived above the shop. Were Sarah and the children upstairs now? Sarah should be here with her husband, but Rose couldn't leave Roman until the paramedics arrived. She prayed that the children wouldn't come down here searching for their father. How old were his children? She tried to remember if Roman had told her. Not that it made any difference. At any age, no child should ever have to witness this.

The ear-splitting sound of sirens nearby buoyed Rose's spirits a fraction.

"It's going to be all right, Roman," she said. Moments later, flashing blue lights reflected through the shop's large front window. The bell on the door tinkled, causing Rose to jump. Momentarily, she released the pressure on the wound before realising what she'd done and reapplying the pressure more firmly.

"What happened?" Two green-suited paramedics filled the cramped space between the shelves.

"He's been stabbed in the stomach." Rose trembled as she related the events to them.

"Ok, love. We'll take over." The cold touch of a plastic glove on her arm made Rose shudder as the paramedic pulled it gently away from the T-shirt.

"It happened about ten minutes ago," Rose said, recovering and forcing herself not to fall apart. Was it only ten minutes? It seemed like hours.

"He's still got a pulse," the female paramedic said. "What's his name, love?"

"Roman Marek. He owns the shop." Rose allowed herself to breathe again. He would be all right now that the professionals were in charge. She should fetch his wife. Sarah should be with him.

"Are you his wife?" The male paramedic stuck a cannula into Roman's arm and held up a bag of fluid, squeezing it to make it flow faster.

"What? No. I'm just a customer."

The female paramedic replaced the T-shirt with a proper dressing. Rose barely noticed her doing it. The T-shirt, now stained bright red, lay discarded on the floor next to Roman. Rose realised, in a daze, she was still wearing nothing over her bra. She grabbed her coat, but before she managed to put it on, a movement across the shop distracted her. Suddenly, the sound of a woman's scream filled the space.

"What's happening?" Sarah Marek appeared from behind the checkout. Rose recognised her from Mum's funeral a few days ago. She must have come down the internal staircase from their flat above the shop.

"Roman?" Sarah collapsed to her knees beside her husband.

"Stand back, love. We're trying to help him." The female paramedic gently took her arm.

Rose approached her. "Sarah." She put a hand on her shoulder to try to comfort her, realising too late her hands were stained with Roman's blood.

Rose fumbled with her coat, trying to put it on quickly before anyone remarked on her state of undress. "I'm really sorry. Some men stabbed your husband, but the paramedics are trying to help him." Rose wanted to tell her it would be all right, but it wasn't up to her to reassure Sarah about that. She glanced in the paramedic's direction, trying to make eye contact, but the woman remained focused on her patient. It didn't bode well that the paramedic seemed stressed beneath her calm exterior.

The external door opened again and two police officers entered.

Rose took charge, needing something to do to stop her from breaking down completely. She repeated all the information she knew. "His name's Roman Marek. He owns the shop. This is his wife, Sarah. Roman got stabbed by two men about fifteen minutes ago." She noticed with relief the cameras above the checkout area. Perhaps she wouldn't need to get too involved. "It should be on the CCTV."

"The CCTV doesn't work," Sarah said. "It got broken, and it cost too much to replace." She sobbed quietly into her hands, barely able to look at her husband.

"I'm sure it won't matter," Rose said, trying to reassure her.

Sarah clutched at Rose's arm. "My children are upstairs. Please, can you fetch a neighbour to take care of them? I'll need to go to the hospital with Roman."

"Of course." Rose would be relieved to step outside for a few minutes. The intense atmosphere inside the shop was becoming hard to bear.

"She's at number 56. Her name's Maggie Mahoney. Please ask her to come quickly."

Rose squeezed Sarah's hand. "I'll get her," she said.

One of the police officers tried to prevent her from leaving. "You need to stay here. You're a witness."

"I need to fetch someone to mind the Mareks' children." She glared at him angrily, not willing to take no for an answer. "I'll be five minutes." She quickly gave her name and address to the police officer, opening the door before he changed his mind.

Once Rose got out onto the street, she realised how much darker the evening had become since she entered the shop. The street lighting along this stretch of road didn't seem to work, making it almost pitch-black. At first, she worried that the two men may still be lurking nearby and see her come out, but she dismissed the idea as totally irrational. Those men would be long gone. She fastened her coat and walked as fast as possible in the dark.

Number 56 was only a few doors along. Rose rang the doorbell, painfully aware of her blood-covered hands and the dirty red smudges adorning her coat.

A large woman with curlers in her hair answered the door.

"Are you Maggie Mahoney?" Rose asked. "Sarah Marek sent me." Quickly, she explained that Roman had been stabbed and Sarah needed someone to take care of the children so she could go with him to hospital.

A few minutes later, Rose returned with Maggie, filling her in with some of the details during the rushed walk back to the shop.

The paramedics were loading Roman into the ambulance. To Rose's relief, he still appeared to be alive.

A tearful Sarah ran up to them. She thrust a door key into Maggie's hand. "The children are upstairs. Please take care of them. Don't tell them anything about this. Tell them Mummy will be back soon." She ran to the ambulance, climbing inside. The door shut behind her, pulling away shortly afterwards amid the blare of sirens.

Rose shivered. The shock finally hit her with a big punch in the guts, so that she longed for a shoulder to cry on. Right now, even Philip, her estranged husband, would be better than no one, but he lived miles away in Manchester. "You should see to the children," she urged Maggie, who seemed to be frozen in disbelief. "There's nothing you can do here."

Maggie took a deep breath and came to her senses. "Yes, of course. Don't worry, I'll take good care of them."

Rose couldn't help worrying. Even though she had never met the children, she imagined how she would feel if it was her son, Jack, if he was still a child, waking up from the noise out on the street to find his parents missing, and one of them seriously injured.

"We need to talk to you." A voice behind Rose startled her. This entire experience caused her to be extra jumpy. She turned, coming face to face with the police officer who had tried to stop her from leaving the shop earlier. More than anything, she wanted to go straight home, pour a large glass of gin, and watch something on TV to take her mind off this evening's awful events. She didn't have any gin and still didn't have any milk either, so she couldn't even make a decent cup of tea.

"You were in the shop when the attack took place." It didn't come out as a question.

Rose nodded, wondering what she should tell the police.

"What exactly happened?" The police officer poised over her notebook with a pen.

"I was at the far end of the shop." It wasn't as if she'd really seen anything. "Looking for milk and butter," she added. She guessed the police wouldn't let her back into the shop now to buy a loaf of bread, either. She would have nothing for breakfast tomorrow. On the plus side, her twenty-pound note remained untouched.

"Then what happened?" The officer prompted her.

"Two men came in. They demanded money from Roman. He said he didn't have it." The men were threatening, frighteningly so. She'd hidden at the far end of the shop like a coward. However bad she felt about that now, it proved to be the right thing to do. It might easily have been her who got stabbed.

"Can you describe the men?" The officer looked up from her notebook, staring Rose right in the eye as if daring her to lie about any of it.

"I didn't see them. I hid in the far corner of the shop."

The officer's face dropped.

Whatever Rose said now, truthfully, she couldn't describe either of the men well enough to be of any use in identifying them as she only caught a few glimpses in the edge of the security mirror. She certainly didn't see either of their faces. They might have been anybody. Quickly, she replayed the events in her mind. She might recognise their voices, and maybe she'd caught a few minor details: a black leather jacket, a wisp of brown hair, a bulky figure. Reliving the attack in her head made her feel vulnerable and even more frightened. She was certain the men didn't see her. If they had, they would have confronted her instead of leaving her to be a witness. If she stopped talking now, she would be safe. Those men would never realise she'd been in the shop. If she made a big thing of it, remembered every last detail, sooner or later those men would find out about her involvement. Rose understood the risks from her experience with Jordan Taylor, her mother's murderer, and she refused to put herself through that experience again.

"Anything else? Even the tiniest thing might help."

"I don't remember any more." Rose's voice shook as she spoke.

"You must have heard them speak. What did they say?"

"I couldn't make out any words. They spoke too quietly." She wouldn't tell them one of the men was named Terry. *Don't get involved. The police can't protect you.*

"What did they sound like? Did they have an accent? Were they young or old?"

Rose pretended to mull over the question for a few seconds. The two voices still echoed around in her head, like a bad earworm that she would never get rid of.

"They were just average," she said. Was that the truth? The truth was, she was a middle-aged woman living alone in an undesirable area. The truth was, she needed to do what it took to survive, even though she hated herself for it.

The other officer came out of the shop, looking serious. "Roman Marek died on the way to hospital," he said.

Chapter 4

Rose gasped at the news of Roman's death. "That's awful." She caught sight of her hands, still stained with his blood from her pointless attempt to help him. Now she just wanted to get home and wash everything off. She longed to scrub at her hands until every last trace of this evening's violence melted away. Her thoughts turned to Sarah Marek and the two children Rose had never met. Should she try to tell the police officer what she knew, for their sake? Surely, she ought to do everything in her power to prevent a murderer from going free, to not let him win.

"So it's a murder enquiry now," the female officer said. "I get why they call this area the Murder Mile. Is that the third one, or the fourth in the last few months?"

"I think it might be the fifth," her colleague said.

Rose shuddered. The Murder Mile? That sounded horrendous. Wasn't this supposed to be a nice neighbourhood? Yes, the area was poor but friendly and with a sense of community, not somewhere innocent people got killed. Yet, her own mother was murdered less than five minutes from here. Was she number three or number four? Was that all her mother meant to the police? A number. A shocking statistic.

"I don't suppose we'll catch the person responsible, not if it's a gang killing. They'll all close ranks and no one will dare to talk." The officer didn't seem to be in a hurry to do anything useful.

"Maybe not, but the Murder Investigation Team will still expect us to do all the grunt work. Have you called them?" The officer tucked in a strand of hair that was coming loose in the breeze.

"Yep. They're on their way. I'm not mad keen on doing house-to-house enquiries around here." The police officer looked at his watch as if he needed to be somewhere else. "You know how much the people on this estate hate the police."

"It'll be ok. We'll do it as a pair. It's not safe to split up."

23

Rose coughed to remind them of her existence. "Can I go home now?" All that talk about murder put the heebie-jeebies up her. The sooner she got back to the flat and locked the door behind her, the safer she would feel.

"Are you sure you can't remember anything else?" the female officer asked.

Rose hesitated as the police officers' talk of gangs whirled around in her head. Gangs were a problem in Manchester, too. Thankfully, not in the pleasant area where she had lived, but she heard a lot of rumours, especially about the extreme level of violence towards anyone who grassed on them. The police must have some idea who was responsible. Surely, they would find enough evidence to catch and convict the murderer without her getting embroiled in this mess. But what if they didn't? What if the man who stabbed Roman Marek remained free? What if the stuff she already told the police wasn't enough? Self-preservation kicked in, telling her to stay out of it. She shouldn't ignore her instinct, for Jack's sake, if not her own.

"No," she said firmly. "I've told you everything I can remember."

"The Murder Investigation Team will want to talk to you. They'll be in touch."

At least that would give Rose some time to get her story straight and plan what to tell them. They didn't need her. There would be CCTV, if not in the shop, then somewhere nearby. The two attackers would be caught on camera somewhere. Or they would have left DNA traces. There were so many tools the police could use to investigate these days. They didn't need to put her at risk. But those thoughts did nothing to quell the guilt building up inside her.

Rose walked briskly towards her new home. In less than five minutes, she opened the main door to the block and ran up the three flights of communal stairs in her desperation to make it to the safety of the flat. She fumbled with her key in the lock, puffing heavily. Eventually, the door clicked open. Hurriedly, she banged it shut behind her, leaned against it, and sobbed until her breathing returned to normal.

She still needed to clean herself up. She washed her hands in the bathroom sink to remove the worst of the blood. Mum's toiletries sat on the edge of the bath. She grabbed some shower gel and an almost empty shampoo bottle, another thing she'd need to find some money to buy.

As she undressed, she noticed the blood stains on most of her clothes, where her hands had rubbed against them. She piled them up in the sink, ready to soak them in cold water in the bath when she'd cleaned herself up. Her T-shirt must still be in the shop. She didn't want it back. The total soaking from Roman's blood would have rendered it beyond redemption, even if she could ever bring herself to wear it again.

The bath's shower attachment didn't compare well to the expensive power-shower in her Manchester house. *That life's finished*, she reminded herself. *Stop hankering after the past and make the best of things now.* At least it was serviceable. The warm water eased some of the tension in her muscles. She stayed under it for far too long, worrying that, at some point, she'd have to pay the gas bill. But she felt contaminated. By the time she'd finished, the bottle of shower gel was half-empty, and her hands and forearms were scrubbed red. She still didn't feel completely clean.

Rose set about cleaning the bath, pulling long strands of her brown hair from the plughole, and removing all traces of blood before remembering she needed to soak her stained clothes.

As soon as she finished, she heated up half of the tin of beans, deciding it would be prudent to eke out her few remaining provisions until she managed to get some money. No point in wishing for toast now, not that she had any appetite after this evening's events. Where was the nearest supermarket anyway, assuming Roman Marek's shop would be currently out of bounds, and how would she get there? Roman Marek's shop was sure to be closed tomorrow, at least. It was a crime scene, and from her recent experience, the police wouldn't rush to finish processing it.

With Roman gone, Rose wondered who would run the shop. She gained the impression from her previous stay in Mum's flat that Roman was mostly a one-man band. His passing would leave a gaping hole in the business. His wife certainly wouldn't be in a fit state to take over, not yet, not in the throes of grief, perhaps not ever, with two children to care for, children who had just lost their father and would need plenty of time and attention. Her heart went out to Sarah Marek. What must she be going through now?

Rose slept badly. Guilt. She woke in the night and, for the next few hours, tossed and turned in bed, debating with herself if she should inform the police that one of Roman's attackers was called Terry, or if she should keep quiet to ensure her own safety. The police did nothing to protect her from Jordan Taylor, the man who murdered her mother. How would they protect her from this Terry, and his friend, when they didn't even know their identities? Without his full name, telling the police would do more harm than good.

Chapter 5

Tanya was unlocking the door to go into her flat just as Rose headed out to the job centre the next morning.

"Hiya. How are you settling in?" Tan asked.

The friendly voice warmed Rose after the terrible events of yesterday evening. She tried to smile. The smile didn't make it all the way to her face.

"I..." Should she tell Tan about the stabbing? She didn't want it getting round the neighbourhood that she'd witnessed the entire thing. "I had a dreadful evening." The overwhelming desire to talk to someone loosened her tongue before she could stop it. At least she hadn't said anything specific.

"You look all in." Tan pushed open her door. "Come in for a cuppa."

This time, the corners of Rose's lips managed a tiny upturn. The craving for a cup of tea with milk proved even stronger than the desire to talk to someone. "That would be lovely." The job centre would wait. It would probably mean queueing for a little longer when she got there, but time was one commodity she possessed in plenty at the moment.

Tan ushered her inside, leading her into the kitchen, which, in sharp contrast to Rose's flat, appeared to be almost brand-new. Rose guessed Tan must be a council tenant, so the council would have paid to modernise the flat, probably just before she moved in. Most of the properties on this estate were still in council ownership. Her mother was one of the fortunate few who had bought her flat.

"Where did you move from?" Rose asked.

"Other side of Brackford. We lived there, like forever." Tan pulled a couple of teabags out of an earthenware container. "Council put me in the Brackford flat when I got preggers with Darren."

"Why the move?" Brackford seemed to be a much nicer area, so moving here made no sense to Rose.

"Trouble with the neighbours," Tan snapped, turning her back on Rose to get the milk from the fridge.

Rose changed the subject. "How old is Darren now?" She didn't need a noisy young kid living nearby.

"He's twenty-two."

Rose's face lit up with relief. "I've got a son too. Jack's nineteen. He's at university."

"Lucky you. Wish Darren would move out, not that he's here much. Only comes home when he needs feeding or his washing done." The kettle clicked off, and Tan poured water into two mugs. "How do you like your tea?"

"Milk, no sugar, please."

Tan put the steaming mugs on the small dining table in the kitchen and pulled out a chair, indicating for Rose to do the same.

"What happened last night, then? Your dreadful evening?"

Rose took a sip of her tea to give herself a moment to think. It burnt her lip. She set the mug back on the table, still tempted by the glorious sight of milky tea, to gulp it down, despite its scalding temperature. "The shopkeeper down the road got stabbed," Rose spoke slowly, still trying to work out how to present the story, in order to come out of it without alerting anyone to the fact that she witnessed the entire thing.

"What, the Polish guy?" Tan got up and took a half-open packet of biscuits from a nearby cupboard. She offered one to Rose. "I met him yesterday lunchtime."

"Roman Marek, yes," she said, disconcerted that Tan didn't appear at all shocked by the news of a murder practically on her doorstep. "He died on the way to hospital," she added, in case she hadn't made it clear.

Tan remained calm. "That's awful. What happened?"

Rose shook her head. "I don't know. I found him. I went out for some milk, but when I went into the shop he was sprawled out on the floor bleeding." It wasn't exactly a lie, but the subtle omission of the truth ought to be enough to keep her safe.

"That's awful. Poor you." Tan offered her another biscuit.

"Yes, it was dreadful." Rose nibbled at the biscuit, wondering how many she could snaffle down without appearing rude. A couple more might last her beyond lunchtime.

"He told me about his wife and kids yesterday. I'm sure I got his entire life history, even his move here from Poland with his parents. His family must be distraught."

"Yes, Sarah, his wife, is so nice. She doesn't deserve that."

"Those poor girls." Tan shook her head sadly. "He said they both went to the local primary school. That's much too young to lose a parent."

Rose agreed. She had worried about them all night. In her head, they'd been teenagers. Finding out they were very much younger shocked her, almost made her want to come clean to the police and tell them every last little detail. Rose immediately reset the pictures in her head to make the children miniature copies of Sarah Marek. It didn't make her feel any better. Losing a parent at any age was traumatic. Even for herself, at the age of forty-four, losing her mother recently hadn't proved easy, particularly coming right on top of the double whammy of discovering her husband's affair and getting fired from her job.

She took a gulp of her tea, now suitably cooled. After a day of milkless tea, it tasted divine.

"Can I ask you a question?" It had been buzzing around Rose's head all night, along with the other atrocities of yesterday evening. Tan might know the answer if she'd lived in Brackford for over twenty years.

"Course you can, love."

"The police referred to this place as the Murder Mile. They said lots of people have been murdered in the area."

Tan laughed. "That's a load of rubbish. Just something the local pa-per invented to jazz up a story and sell more copies. Gives this place a bad name. It's not even a mile. They should have measured it properly, got their facts right."

It didn't bode well if Rose wanted to sell the flat. What would a reputation like that do to property prices in the area? "What about the other murders?" Since yesterday, Rose felt even less safe here now. She was thankful she'd got a decent lock fitted on Mum's door recently.

"There's been three. That's probably no more than any other area of North-East London," Tan said. "Forget about it. Would I move here if it was that bad?"

Rose was still unsure. She vaguely recalled hearing some statistic that only a few hundred murders occurred in the whole of the UK every year, so three murders in a small area constituted a relatively huge number. But statistics could prove, or disprove, anything, depending on how you interpreted them. Three was still a small number. Small enough to be a coincidence? She wasn't convinced.

"Tell me about the others," Rose said. "I'm beginning to wonder if this is a safe area to live in."

Tan laughed. "You want to stop worrying. You'll be fine here. It's mostly gang stuff. The gang's got no beef with you, so they won't bother you. You don't give them any trouble, they won't give you any."

"Ok." Tan's reassurance did nothing to quell the nausea in her stomach. Jordan Taylor certainly had a lot of beef with her. It had been the right decision to stay out of this murder business, although she may have already said too much. She only hoped none of the police officers who questioned her last night would leak her name to the wrong per-son. Roman Marek had been murdered for protection money, so Rose had inadvertently got herself involved with the local gangs for the sec-ond time this month and put herself right in the firing line.

Deciding she needed to economise and save the bus fare, the walk to the job centre took nearly forty minutes. It came as a shock to Rose how out of shape she'd become. Perhaps a lack of exercise explained why she'd put on a few pounds lately. She would love a sit-down and another cup of tea to recover before the return walk, but no chance of that.

The queue to speak with an advisor moved at a painfully slow pace. When she finally got to talk to someone, the woman was very little help, simply gave her a ton of forms to fill in and told her it would be several weeks before she actually received any money and, if she failed to apply for any jobs, she would lose her benefits.

Rose left the building feeling very despondent. She didn't want benefits. She wanted a job, something that would make her independent, not leave her at the mercy of a bunch of officious pen-pushers who could take everything away from her on a whim.

Rose agonised for ages over whether she should visit Sarah Marek. Now, stood on Sarah's doorstep, she still wasn't certain she was doing the right thing. She knocked tentatively on the door of the Mareks' flat. The shop had been closed all day, but she'd seen Sarah at the upstairs window when she walked past on her way to the job centre.

Part of her didn't want to intrude on Sarah's grief. But her morning at the job centre proved a complete waste of time. It should be easy to find a job, given that she couldn't afford to be fussy. But she either lacked the necessary qualifications or experience, or she was overqualified, or she was unsuitable in some other way. Ironically, she would be forced to apply for a minimum number of these jobs she wasn't suitable for or risk losing her benefits—the benefits she wouldn't actually get for several weeks, by the time they processed all the paperwork. So much for the efficiency of government departments. In the meantime, how would she pay her bills? They weren't very helpful about that when she'd asked. At least she didn't have to pay rent or a mortgage, but she did need to eat and keep paying her monthly phone bill, so she needed to earn some money fast.

In Rose's opinion, Sarah Marek needed help, and Rose had the time to give it to her. Her idea might solve both of their problems.

She knocked at the door again, louder this time, in case her initial knock went unheard. What if Sarah didn't want to be disturbed? Rose wouldn't blame her for wanting to be left alone. Roman's violent death must be a massive shock. Rose understood that better than anyone, following her mother's murder so recently. It would take time for the event to even sink in. If Sarah didn't answer the door this time, Rose would leave her be and try again tomorrow.

The click of a key turning in the lock got her hopes up. A few seconds later, the door opened a crack. Rose spotted the chain still on the door. It was understandable that Sarah would be security conscious after yesterday's events.

"It's Rose. Do you remember? From yesterday." Rose wondered if Sarah would recognise her. It was only the second time they ever met, and both meetings were brief. Sarah must have been in shock for those few minutes when their paths crossed in the shop. It would be perfectly reasonable if she'd forgotten. "I'm sorry to intrude on you at this time, but I'd like to help you."

The door closed, then, a second later, opened wide.

"That's very nice of you, but honestly, if anyone brings me another casserole, I think I'll scream."

Rose held her hands out to prove she had arrived casserole-less. As if she could afford to give away good food right now.

"I'm sorry. I'm really not feeling very sociable at the moment. I'm not sure what I'm going to do," Sarah said.

"I'm sorry too," Rose said. "I only met Roman a few times. He was very kind to me. It must be dreadful for you."

"I don't know how I'm going to cope with the children and everything."

"What about the shop?" Rose asked, conscious of jumping into the dead man's shoes before his body was even cold. "Have you got anyone to help you with the shop?"

"Roman has an assistant, but he only works part time. Roman worked so many hours in that shop. I take care of the children, so it was mostly just him."

Rose smiled weakly. "I would like to help you," she said. "I need a job desperately, and it sounds like you need someone to work in the shop. I only moved here this week and I've got no income."

Sarah stared at her blankly. Rose wondered if she was contemplating her offer, or if, like herself, she considered it an insensitive bloody cheek to be mentioning the subject so soon. "I would love to work in the shop," Rose continued, eager to get through to Sarah before she shut the door in her face. "I'm willing to work any hours you need." Let's face it, she had nothing else to do in her spare time. No husband, no friends, no life.

"I'm not sure," Sarah said. "Do you have any experience of running a shop?"

Absolutely nothing. "I've worked in offices and I'm good at getting on with people. I know all about ordering stock, stuff like that. And I can probably help with the accounts." She lacked expertise in any of those things, but a bit of research on the internet would soon change that, and she was willing to blag it in order to get the job. "Why not give me a test run for a week? See how it goes. It would be better than shutting the shop." She guessed Sarah would need the income the business provided. Had that occurred to Sarah yet, or was she too grief-stricken to care?

Rose surmised from Sarah's expression that the practicalities were only now dawning on her.

"When does your assistant work? If I start when he's available, he can show me a few things, then I can manage on my own." Rose didn't want to give Sarah a chance to say no. She felt bad pressurising her, but it would be for her own good in the long run.

"He normally comes in a couple of days a week and early evenings so that Roman can spend some time with the family. I'll have to phone him to check if he can come in for an extra couple of hours to show you what to do."

Rose smiled. Sarah appeared to be almost sold on the idea.

"Are you sure you want to take this on?"

The unspoken words, *after what happened yesterday*, hung in the air. Truthfully, Rose wasn't sure at all, but desperation forced her to continue. Surely those men wouldn't come back a second time. They would be too worried about being caught. The shop would probably be the safest place in the neighbourhood right now.

"I'll be fine," Rose said. "Please, will you let me try? I won't let you down." If Sarah said no, then Rose would literally have no money for several weeks. She would struggle to buy food, let alone anything else. The only option left to her would be to go back to the job centre and beg, fill in all the extra paperwork, jump through all the hoops they placed in the way as if she were a toy poodle. She would rather work for her money.

"Give me your phone number. I'll arrange for Roman's assistant to come in and give you some training. When can you start?"

Rose smiled. "I can start now."

"It's still a crime scene. The police won't let anyone go in yet. But they say they'll be finished by the end of today."

"How about tomorrow morning? I don't mind coming in early to clean everything up."

"Are you sure you want to do that? It's not a nice job."

"Yes, I'm sure," Rose said, even though she agreed with Sarah. It would be a horrible job. But it would be far worse to expect Sarah to do it. She handed over her phone number.

"As soon as you need me, you call. Anytime." If she didn't get a call tomorrow, she'd need to start searching for another job. That would be easier said than done. She remembered the reference problem. She'd been sacked. Her old company wouldn't give her a good reference. If she was lucky, Sarah wouldn't ask her for one. She hoped Sarah realised how much this job meant to her, but she didn't want to put any more pressure on her now.

A small girl appeared in the doorway and wrapped her arms around Sarah's legs.

"Is this one of your daughters?" Rose asked, smiling at her.

"Yes, this is Chloe."

She looked so young. It made Roman's death even more tragic. "Hello, Chloe," she said. "My name's Rose."

Chloe smiled shyly, then hid her face behind her mother's leg.

"How old are you?" Rose asked.

"I'm six," Chloe said softly.

Rose's heart melted. "I'll leave you to it. Can I do anything else for you?"

"No, thank you, everyone's been so good. The whole neighbourhood's rallied round."

"That's nice," Rose said. Maybe this wasn't such a terrible place, after all. Though she guessed everyone would be keen to help this week. But next week, offers of help would tail off to nearly nothing. She hoped Sarah would find some inner resilience and get over the worst of her grief quickly. It must be tough having to be strong for two young children who probably didn't fully understand what had happened to their daddy.

"Please phone me as soon as you've spoken to your assistant," Rose said. "I really do want to help, and I'm in dire need of a job. I'm sure I can do this." She would need to be tough. Last night, and most of to-day, she'd suffered from flashbacks, vivid pictures of Roman's body lying on the floor, covered in blood, so much blood. It occurred to her that something similar might happen again. Perhaps Sarah would increase security if she could find the money to do it, although Rose assumed money would be tighter now, with the main breadwinner in the Marek family gone, and Sarah having to pay Rose's wages.

Rose walked back to the flat. At least it wouldn't be a long com-mute to work. But she would probably need to work some evenings. The shop would carry on staying open late. It would never survive with-out it, not against competition from the big supermarkets. She didn't relish the prospect of walking home at eleven o'clock at night. But she would have to, or she would let Sarah down, as well as plummeting straight back to square one with no job and no money. A tear rolled down her cheek. She wiped it away and steeled herself to be tough. She was done crying. Everything had gone so horribly wrong for her lately, things simply couldn't get any worse. Now she must concentrate on fix-ing her problems.

As soon as she got home, she would phone Jack. He might answer this time. Rose longed to talk to him, but what would she say? She still needed to tell him about her and Philip splitting up, and she refused to do that over the phone.

She probably should talk to Philip about it before he ploughed ahead and told Jack the news in a phone call. He wouldn't even con-sider that to be a bad idea. She couldn't face talking to Philip now. She would try Jack first. Speaking to her son always cheered her up. Maybe then she would feel up to calling Philip.

It occurred to her that right now, nobody really knew or cared where she was. That might have been *her* yesterday in that shop. If she died, would anybody miss her? Philip wouldn't care. And no one here would have a contact number for Jack. Jack didn't know yet about her move here. Her old friends weren't aware she'd left Manchester. And, of course, her mum was gone.

So, it was just her and her beloved son, who barely made any time to talk to her, unable to drag himself away from student life and all the sports teams he played on at weekends. How did her existence come to this? Stuck with living alone in this crappy place.

Things could only get better. And she needed to make the best of it because right now she didn't see any way out of this mess. She always told Jack the same thing. Make the best of things. Take your opportunities when you can. Mothers were expected to say those things. Did she really believe it? Well, she needed to be a good role model for Jack even if he would rarely visit her to see it. She needed to show him how to rise up like a phoenix out of the ashes, even though the fire still burned ferociously. That's what she would do. She would be a phoenix. Somehow, she would rise up out of this mess.

Chapter 6

Rose got up early and arrived at the shop as Sarah was unlocking. Sarah planned to introduce her to her other employee. He would show her the ropes, and they would work out a rota between them. Rose hoped her new colleague would be someone she could get on with.

It would be good to earn some money—one less problem to worry about. She wondered if Sarah would give her an advance on her wages, but probably day one wouldn't be the greatest time to ask. She would broach the subject later in the week. Poor Sarah had enough to contend with at the moment without being harassed for money by a new employee. She barely seemed to be holding herself together. Rose wasn't surprised. It must be a terrible shock for her losing her husband so suddenly and in such a dreadful way.

"Come in." Sarah switched the sign on the shop door to *open*. "I hope we get some customers today. I'm worried our regulars may have gone somewhere else while we were closed. Perhaps they'll be too frightened to come back."

Rose sensed Sarah trembling as she spoke. She longed to send the poor woman home, but they would have to wait until her co-worker arrived.

"I'm sure everyone will want to come in to support you," Rose said. More likely, they would come for the novelty value, to see where Roman got stabbed to death.

"I'm worried about that too." Tears started to trickle down Sarah's face. "Sorry. I can't help it. I keep thinking of Roman."

"How are you coping?" *Stupid question.* "It must be tough for you." Rose was struggling enough with her own emotions. It must be so much harder for Sarah.

"I'm trying to be brave for the children, but it's so difficult."

Rose wondered whether to give her a hug or if that might make her break down completely. What must the poor woman be going through? "Children can be very resilient," Rose said. Was that true in a case like this? She'd thankfully never known any young children who'd lost their father in such awful circumstances, but it seemed like the right thing to say.

Would Jack be equally resilient when she broke the news to him about her and Philip splitting up? It hardly compared. Perhaps she would remind him of that if he kicked up a fuss. Jack was no longer a child, which made the situation worse because he understood all the implications, so he would fight against it more.

"I really hope so," Sarah said, dabbing her eyes with a tissue.

"If I can do anything to help, you only have to ask." Everybody said that, but Rose really did mean it. "And, if you want to talk, I understand what you're going through." From her own experience, coming to terms with murder was infinitely more traumatic than going through a normal bereavement. She was about to say she'd got the T-shirt, then remembered her own T-shirt, soaked with Roman's blood, and shut up.

"Thank you. That's really kind, but you're doing more than enough already. I can't possibly keep the shop going on my own and I need the income to support the girls."

"It's helping me too," Rose said. "I need an income as well." Best to remind Sarah tactfully that she would need paying. She wasn't doing this out of the goodness of her heart. She was doing it to survive. At this stage, she probably should insist on having a proper contract of employment. But this wasn't the time to mention it. And cash in hand might be better after all, as the money wouldn't go far, not on the minimum wage rate Sarah suggested. It would be enough to get by, and that would have to do for now.

Rose still felt partly responsible, even though Roman's murder wasn't her fault in the slightest. She should have helped him more, done something to prevent him from being stabbed, as if she could have flown out like a ninja and performed some sort of clever karate move, knocking both of Roman's attackers out cold on the floor without breaking into a sweat. Even in her wildest dreams, that would never happen, and no one would expect it of her. If she'd moved from her hiding place, she might have been the one to be stabbed instead. There was no logic to her guilt. But logic had nothing to do with it.

Maybe the effects of PTSD were catching up with her. She hadn't slept well again last night, constantly fighting images of blood and knives, with everything exaggerated to make the dream even worse than the stark reality.

"Alfie should be here soon," Sarah said. "He can show you round, and he's promised to stay all morning to teach you everything you need to know."

"That's great." The prospect of a few hours of training before flying solo put Rose more at ease, although how difficult could it be to manage a small shop? Chat with the customers, take the money, restock the shelves every now and again. Easy, right? Until a customer comes in with a knife and a bad attitude.

Rose shuddered. If the experience really had resulted in PTSD, she'd never be able to cope with working here. Why hadn't she considered that before now? She told herself to toughen up and get on with the job, because honestly, her choices were severely limited. Without money, she would starve, which may be a worse way to go than a quick knife wound to the stomach.

The bell above the door tinkled, signalling someone entering. Rose's heart rate automatically quickened. How long would it take her to get over that feeling of trepidation every time a new customer arrived?

"Alfie." Sarah greeted the man who entered.

"How are you, darling?"

Sarah's face fell and Rose worried the tears would start flowing again. She recalled from her own experience, it didn't take much to set them off.

Alfie gave Sarah a big hug. "Don't you worry, darling. I'll sort out the shop." He turned to Rose. "You must be Rose. Nice to meet you."

Alfie Cooper wasn't a bit like Rose imagined. He probably should be retired, with his craggy face and grey hair. At least, his small remaining patch of hair was grey. But, in sharp contrast, his body seemed surprisingly fit and muscular. Rose suddenly felt safer, until she remembered they'd be sharing out the hours to run the shop between them, so they'd rarely be present at the same time.

Alfie smiled broadly at her, giving the impression of a loveable charmer. Then he gave Sarah another hug. "You go upstairs, darling, take care of those kiddies. I'll sort out Rose, show her the ropes."

Rose smiled. She could use a light-hearted, fun morning after the events of the last couple of weeks: discovering Philip's affair, being fired from her job, her mother's murder, getting attacked by her mother's killer, and now witnessing another violent murder. It was a miracle she'd survived everything so far. "Yes, don't worry, Sarah. I'm sure Alfie will look after me."

"Thank you." Sarah appeared relieved.

Rose wondered if the children would still be in bed, as it was only just gone 7:00 a.m. Best if Sarah got back to them before they woke up.

"So where do we start?" Rose asked Alfie as soon as Sarah left.

"Soon as we get a customer, I'll show you how to work the till." Alfie flashed a smile at her. "Meanwhile, we should start with a cup of tea."

He showed her around the shop, pointing out some of the things she would be required to do regularly, like checking the sell-by dates of items, keeping the fridge clean and maintaining a daily log of its temperature, and watching out for anyone at the far end of the shop trying to steal the stock.

"Is shoplifting a big problem?" Rose asked.

"Hell yes." Alfie smiled. "You need eyes in the back of your head to work here."

Alfie stayed for three hours to train Rose, then pronounced her competent. Before going home, he left her strict instructions to phone him if she encountered the slightest problem. To her enormous surprise, she coped remarkably well and didn't need to phone him at all. By the time he returned at 6:00 p.m., Rose was nearly dropping off with exhaustion.

Tan came out of her flat as Rose trudged up the stairs. "I've been watching out for you," she said. "Come in. You must be knackered. I'll make you a cup of tea, and you can put your feet up and relax."

"That sounds wonderful." Rose didn't feel capable of lifting a finger right now. How would she cope with doing this every day? Her previous job involved sitting down most of the time, but running the shop entailed more physical work, in between the periods of sitting. She reminded herself of her lack of choice. It was this or nothing, and at least she enjoyed being in charge and meeting lots of new people.

Chapter 7

Tan ushered Rose into her living room. "Make yourself comfortable. I'll bring you a cuppa in a minute. Milk, no sugar, isn't it?"

Rose sat down. She'd been longing to take the weight off her feet for the last couple of hours. She'd restocked all the shelves in between customers, wanting to prove herself to Alfie. She really needed this job.

Tan came back quickly with two steaming mugs of tea. "So how did your first day go?" Tan sat down next to her.

"I never realised how busy that little shop would get." Seriously, Rose imagined she would get a couple of customers every hour, but when she added things up, two customers an hour wouldn't even begin to pay her wages. "It's tiring, but I expect I'll get used to it, and I loved it."

"That's good." Tan took a gulp of her tea.

"It's amazing how much you find out about the community. Everyone wants to talk." *Perhaps, eventually, someone would let slip the name of the person who murdered Roman Marek.*

"It does seem to be the hub of the community, not that I know anything. I've only lived here for a couple of days," Tan said.

Rose finished her tea quickly. It would be nice not to have to get up again all evening, but she didn't want to outstay her welcome. "I'd better get going. You must be expecting Darren back soon."

Tan laughed. "You must be joking. I hardly ever see Darren. Most of the time, he only comes home when he wants a good meal or his washing done. I reckon he's got a girlfriend. It's a pity she doesn't do laundry. You stay as long as you like, love, as long as you're gone by the time I need to go to work."

"You work nights?" That explained why she'd seen Tan appearing to go into her flat very early in the mornings.

"Yep. I'm like you, take what I can get when I can get it."

"What do you do?"

"Oh, nothing exciting. Customer services."

"I'm going to visit my son, Jack, on Saturday next week." Rose had nearly forgotten, what with her new job, but she was so excited at the prospect of seeing Jack.

"That's great. He's at university, isn't he? Which one is he at?"

"Essex. He's living in Colchester, so not too far away. It will be much easier to visit now that I'm living here."

"You're lucky. I wish my Darren had gone to university, but no one can afford it these days. Why would he want to get lumbered with a massive student loan when he can be out earning instead?"

"Yes, you're right, but I'd do anything for Jack." Rose agreed with Tan about the student loan. She and Philip had been paying his tuition fees and most of his expenses so he wouldn't clock up a big loan to worry about after he graduated. Not that either of them would be helping him out financially anymore. Jack might well end up with a huge student loan. Money was yet another thing she would need to discuss with him. Silently, she cursed Philip for the millionth time this week.

Tan smiled. "I'd do anything for my Darren, too. Anyway, how did you hit it off with Alfie?"

"He seemed very nice." That had been a very pleasant surprise to Rose. She'd been delighted to find Alfie so easy to work with, not that she'd actually be working with him much. They'd arranged a rota when he'd been in the shop this morning. They would cover the long opening hours between them, with Rose taking the larger proportion. That's what she wanted. Without the money from those extra hours, she would never make ends meet, especially as she still needed to pay off her hefty credit card bill. "He's certainly got a sense of humour."

"Maybe I'll check him out myself on my way to work one evening," Tan said. "I need a good laugh."

"Don't tell him I'm exhausted after one day." She didn't want Alfie assuming she wasn't up to the job, in case Sarah decided to fire her.

"Course not. Don't worry about it. You'll be fine in a few days when you get used to it." Tan picked up the empty mugs. "Another cup?"

"I really should be going, but thanks for the tea and the chat." She liked having a friend nearby, although she wondered if she and Tan ever would have been friends in her previous life in Manchester. Probably not.

Chapter 8

Rose found it difficult to believe it was Wednesday already. It had been a whole week since Roman Marek's murder. She shook the memory from her head, not wanting to feed the bad dreams that haunted her every night.

A constant stream of customers kept the shop busy. After five days, Rose had settled into a routine and felt like an old hand at this job. Even so, by mid-morning, exhaustion took over, and she hadn't even found time to make herself a cup of tea since breakfast.

At last, it quietened down a little. Only one woman remained in the shop. Rose had seen her a few times now, often with a young child in tow. She guessed the child must be at school today.

The bell above the door rang, and two men entered the shop. The larger of the men walked straight up to Rose, who sat at the till.

"Good morning," she said, feigning cheerfulness. She didn't like the look of either man, and something about this big guy made the hairs on the back of her neck stand rigidly to attention. Rose noticed his friend talking to the young woman customer. Moments later, the woman abandoned her basket of shopping on the floor and walked out.

Immediately, Rose began to worry. What was going on? She wished there were a panic button behind the counter. Taking a deep breath, she willed herself to stay calm.

"We've come for our money," the larger of the two men said. He wasn't especially tall, but Rose reckoned he'd top 200lb on the scales. She couldn't decide how much of his bulk consisted of muscle and how much might be fat.

His friend joined him, intimidating Rose further still.

"What money?" Rose asked. She didn't like the sound of this. Her mind flashed back to the day of Roman's murder. Those men had demanded money. Were they the same men, come back to collect their debt? Surely, she would remember them, wouldn't she? She stared at them alternately, hoping some detail might spark a hint of recognition, but nothing about them seemed familiar. Was her memory fading already, or did neither of these men have anything to do with Roman Marek's murder?

The larger man spoke. "Didn't your boss tell you? We collect money every Wednesday. It's an insurance policy, to make sure no one gets hurt." He sneered at her, his fat lower lip reminding her of a slug.

"Which boss?" Rose tried to breathe deeply without being obvious. She needed to stay calm and in control. Her nails dug into the upholstered seat of her chair in her attempt to conceal her shaking hands. Roman had been stabbed last Wednesday. Was that a coincidence? Did these men have some connection to Roman's murder? Was she looking at Roman's murderer right now? She felt herself beginning to sweat and hoped the men wouldn't smell her fear.

Beefy man bent down, bringing his face level with hers. "Polish bloke." He spat the words out disrespectfully. "The one who's usually here."

The man's lack of respect angered Rose. She told herself to stay calm. "If you mean Mr Marek, one of your lot murdered him last week."

The man's expression didn't change. "No idea what you're talking about."

Rose wondered if his statement was genuine. Again, she scrutinised both men, running her eyes up and down their bodies, trying to match the shape of them with the images in her memory, the images that haunted her every night. Then she replayed the voices in her head. Was one of them Terry? She should be able to answer that question. It upset her that she couldn't.

"Someone stabbed him. He bled to death right there." She pointed to the floor where the two men stood. Strictly speaking, it was a lie. Roman died in the ambulance. But she allowed herself some artistic licence in order to make the point to them. "So no, I don't know anything about any money."

"It's two hundred pounds a week, payable every Wednesday."

The cold, blunt delivery of the statement shocked Rose, especially after what she just told him. It was simply a business deal to him. No platitudes about being sorry to learn of Roman's death. These men were animals. No, that was being unfair to animals.

Two hundred a week was an unsustainable amount of money. She had already formed a rough idea of their monthly takings, and by the time Sarah paid her own expenses, and Rose and Alfie got paid, plus all the other costs involved in running a shop, they wouldn't come close to having a spare 800 pounds a month. "There's no way we can afford that," she said firmly. Her anger at this loathsome man galloped rough-shod over her common sense, but she couldn't help herself. "We've lost a lot of customers because of the murder. They're frightened to come in, so takings are much lower, and Mrs Marek has to pay me to work here, now that Mr Marek is dead, so you're wasting your time asking for money. You should go away and sort out the lowlife who stabbed Mr Marek."

Rose surprised herself with her assertiveness. She looked the man in the eye, recalling Alfie's advice to stand up to people and make them respect her. "You should give us a refund. You call it protection money, but where were you when Mr Marek needed protection?"

"Everyone pays," he said, although he seemed to have lost some of his arrogance.

Rose wondered if she was getting through to him. She pushed the point home. "You didn't protect Mr Marek."

"It's a new contract now. I want two hundred pounds."

Rose shook her head, watching him carefully for any sign that he might be carrying a knife. "We can't afford it. I'll give you fifty pounds." She must be mad. Her common sense screamed at her to just hand over the money, except that wasn't possible. Despite the busy morning in the shop, she didn't have two hundred pounds in cash in the till, just a stack of credit card dockets.

"Are you having a laugh? I can't agree to that."

Rose smiled, determined to hold her nerve. She didn't take her eyes off him, still terrified he might reach into his jacket for a knife. "It's ok. I get it. You're not high enough up in the organisation to make a decision. Go away and ask the boss, explain to him it's bad business to bankrupt us because then you won't get anything at all." What was she doing? She shouldn't be aggravating him like this, but the words had slipped out before she could stop herself. Rose dug her fingernails harder into her chair, worried that the impetuous side of her might decide to thump him. It wouldn't be the first time she'd done something stupid like that.

"One hundred and fifty, now."

Rose paused as if calculating the numbers in her head. She hadn't expected him to concede anything. She'd been trying to buy herself time, knowing she couldn't pay him what he asked for, and hoping some more customers might show up and scare the men off. She let him sweat for a few more moments. "Mr Marek's dead." Rose glared at him, becoming braver now that the moral high ground stood in her favour. "One hundred a week."

The man feigned indecision, then suddenly put his hand out towards her. "Done."

Rose tentatively reached for his hand and shook it quickly, keen to let go as soon as possible.

"We're going to let you off, just this once, mind you, as a mark of respect to Mr Marek. But we'll be back next week."

"Thank you. I appreciate that," Rose said. She didn't appreciate it at all, but at least they'd made some concession, even if it only delayed the inevitable. It would give her time to talk to Alfie. He would know what to do about these men.

The two visitors headed towards the door. The younger one hadn't said anything. He just seemed to be some unimportant lackey. The larger man grabbed a bar of chocolate from the shelf as he passed, holding it up for Rose to see. "Thanks for this, love. Hungry work. See you next Wednesday."

As soon as the door closed behind them, Rose burst into tears. She took out her phone and dialled Alfie.

Alfie arrived ten minutes later. Rose had never been more relieved to see him. She'd been struggling to hold things together since the two men left. Luckily, no new customers arrived, or she might have broken down altogether.

"What happened?" Alfie opened the gateway to come behind the till with her. "Are you ok?"

Rose explained about the two men. "They wanted protection money. Do you know anything about that? Did Roman use to pay them?"

Alfie nodded. "It's the local gang, the Wolfpack. They control everything around here. You'll learn that if you stick around much longer. So yes, Roman paid up. Everybody does, otherwise they trash the place, or they threaten your kids."

"That's awful. Can't the police do anything?" It sounded like she'd had a lucky escape. Rose kicked herself for being reckless enough to argue with them.

"The police are worse than useless. They don't even like coming onto the estate these days, not unless there's a whole team of them with riot gear. They only show up when they really have to."

"They're coming back, the two men, I mean. Next Wednesday. They said they'd let us off this week. The man in charge pleaded ignorance about Roman, but I didn't believe him."

"It may have been different gang members last time," Alfie pointed out. "Although Roman mostly used to get the same ones. Will you be all right when they come back?"

"I'll be ok," Rose said, trying to sound as if she really meant it.

"Are you sure?" Alfie looked concerned. "Perhaps I should work Wednesdays in the future, so you don't have to deal with them again."

"They won't hurt me if I give them the money, will they?" It was sweet of Alfie to offer, but Rose realised she had to face her fears, not hide behind Alfie every time she got a problem.

"How much do they want?"

"They asked for two hundred a week," Rose said.

Alfie looked pale. "Can we afford that much?"

Rose smiled. "Oh, we're not paying that much."

Alfie looked worried. "Did you not listen when I said we had to pay?"

"I renegotiated the price. They agreed to half price, one hundred a week."

"Seriously? You got some balls, girl. It sounds like you handled them brilliantly. You're a bloody genius, but you need to be careful next time. Don't mess with these people, however much it costs."

Rose fully intended to be careful. She didn't want to end up like Roman. She didn't want these men to walk all over her, either, or take advantage of Sarah, who still needed to support her children. Alfie hadn't been here. If he had, he'd probably have read the situation the same as she did. Perhaps these men weren't all bad. Did they feel guilty because they were involved in Roman's murder? If they kept coming back, maybe one of them would slip up one day and say something to prove their involvement. Not that she relished the idea of seeing them every week. She didn't doubt that they would use violence next time if they failed to get what they wanted. Rose forced the scenario from her head. It didn't bear thinking about.

"Thanks for coming, Alfie." Rose was grateful to him for dropping everything to come straight here when she'd phoned. She'd been in such a state after those men left. Alfie immediately calmed her down and made her feel safe again.

"No worries, girl. I'll see you at six," Alfie said. That was his usual time to take over from Rose.

After Alfie left, Rose began to question whether she should really have taken this job—long hours, rubbish pay, and still scared stiff on some days of ending up like Roman, stabbed for the sake of a few quid. She'd taken on the job in desperation for some immediate cash, as well as guilt that she failed to save Roman. Being in the shop that evening, watching the attack in the security mirror, somehow seemed to connect her to this place, and to Roman and Sarah. Besides, she admitted, most of the time she loved working here. She'd met so many new people. What would she be doing if not this, aside from sitting alone in her flat?

Rose tried to put the thoughts out of her head. She would be visiting Jack this weekend. Perhaps, after that, she'd feel much better. It was several weeks since she'd last seen her son and she really looked forward to it. Seeing her son would put everything into perspective.

Chapter 9

Jack was waiting outside the ticket office when Rose arrived at Colchester station early on Saturday evening. She gave him a big hug before he pulled away, embarrassed at the public show of affection from his mother.

"How are you getting on? Are you enjoying university life? How's the course?" Rose bombarded him with questions, hardly letting him get a word in anywhere. She'd missed him so much.

"Ok, calm down, Mum. I've booked a restaurant. Let's talk while we're eating dinner. I'm starving.

He led her out of the station. "It's not far. We can walk there in ten minutes."

Rose smiled at him. "You look well." She fancied that Jack had grown in the last few weeks, although he was already over six feet tall. Seeing him really lifted her spirits. Rose relished the prospect of having her son all to herself for a couple of hours, even though she was still undecided on how to broach the subject of Philip and the divorce. The evening may take a downhill turn once she mentioned that. At least she could enjoy the next few minutes, pretending for a while that everything was still normal.

Thankfully, the Italian restaurant Jack chose wasn't too expensive, although, scanning the menu, Rose guessed it would blow most of her remaining wages for the week. It would be worth it, even if she didn't eat for the next few days. She didn't see nearly enough of Jack, and she wanted to spoil him. He certainly couldn't afford to pick up the bill. Rose was already concerned about Jack's student loan, which was likely to grow exponentially now that neither she nor Phillip was in any position to help him financially, unless, she thought cynically, Philip won big on the horses. *Don't be ridiculous*, she told herself. If Philip won anything on the horses, he would blow it straight away on the next race.

Jack tucked into his starter of calamari as if he hadn't eaten all week. Rose wondered if he did eat properly. His degree, sports science, included plenty of practical sessions, and the students were expected to participate in multiple sports in their spare time, so he needed a ton of energy. He needed to eat well.

"This is great, Mum. Are you sure you don't want some? You can try a mouthful of mine."

It did look delicious. Rose loved calamari. She'd decided to skip a starter for herself to save the money, under the pretence of being on a diet. She shook her head. "Thanks, but you eat it." He needed it more than she did. Besides, she was too distracted, wondering how to tackle the subject of Philip, still trying to pluck up the courage to spit out the words.

Jack shovelled a calamari ring into his mouth. "How's Manchester?"

Rose hesitated.

Jack looked up from his food. "What's up?"

"I need to tell you some things." Rose glanced across the restaurant to check if their main courses were on the way, a distraction that would allow her to delay the inevitable for a few minutes longer. Reluctantly, she pushed that thought away. She should heed Tan's advice and face her fears.

"I've left Manchester." There, she'd said it, even if she'd missed off the vital piece of information about splitting from Philip.

"What about Dad?" Jack suspended his fork in mid-air. A piece of calamari fell from it onto the plate, splattering tomato sauce onto the pristine white tablecloth.

"I've left your father. I'm living in Gran's flat."

"Why?"

Rose watched Jack trying to process the information. She gave him some time.

"Why would you do that? You can't leave him."

"I didn't have a choice," Rose said.

Jack took another mouthful of calamari, then spoke with his mouth full. "Is this some sort of midlife crisis?"

Rose instinctively wanted to remind him of his manners. She stopped herself before the words left her lips. "Of course not."

"Have you got another man? Have you been unfaithful to Dad? I can't believe you would do that." He said it in a way that made it clear that he obviously could, and did, believe it.

Rose was disconcerted by how easily her son could think the worst of her. "No, no, I have never been unfaithful to your father." *For all the good that did me.*

"Then why did you leave him?" He stared at her petulantly. He was still of an age when he viewed life in black and white, when he lacked awareness of the many nuances of grey that shaded real-life situations. There were considerably more than fifty of them.

"I didn't have any choice. He's moved in with another woman." There was no way to sugarcoat that piece of information. She might as well be blunt. Besides, she needed to defend herself. This wasn't her fault.

"Another woman. That's impossible. Dad wouldn't. Who is it? Did you drive him to it? You do nag sometimes."

As if she didn't feel shitty enough about the situation already. *Thanks, Jack.*

"You can make it up with him. You need to go back home and put this right. Please, Mum."

"I can't."

"Please, Mum, go back to Manchester."

Jack's eyes glistened. He wouldn't cry. He rarely did. This time, the tears almost bubbled up to the surface, but Jack kept a tight lid on his well of tears, and he'd long since lost the key to unlock it.

"Why do you want to live in Gran's flat when you've got a much nicer house in Manchester?" He snapped his head up, like something had twanged in his brain. "Has Dad moved the other woman in with him? Is that why you can't stay in our house?"

"No, he's living at her house," Rose said.

"So you should go back and live in our house. At least if you're nearby, you might make things up with him. He'll soon get bored with this other woman and realise he's made a mistake."

Rose noted his desperation and longed to tell him everything would be all right, that Mummy would make it better, but Jack was too old for fairy stories, and she didn't possess a magic wand. "There is no house," she said. "Not anymore. The banks foreclosed on the mortgage. They repossessed it last week."

"Why? There must be some mistake. You both earned good money, didn't you?"

Rose nodded. "It's not that simple," she said.

"It totally is. This isn't something that would have happened overnight. You must have had plenty of time to do something about it. Why didn't you even warn me?"

Yes, Rose thought, there should have been plenty of time to do something about it. *Unless your money is being sucked into a bottomless pit, and your head is buried so deep down in the sand, you can't see the bleeding obvious even when it's right in front of you.* "I didn't even know," Rose said. "Your dad didn't warn me." She hadn't wanted to see the problem. Now that she reflected on it, there had been subtle clues. She had preferred to ignore them, to avoid facing the unthinkable, in case voicing the question would make the inevitable answer true.

"This can't all be Dad's fault. You need to take some of the responsibility."

"It is your dad's fault." It hurt her that Jack was trying so hard to make her the fall guy for Philip's failings. "I'm sorry, darling. I know you love your dad." Philip had always been Jack's favourite, ever since he used to take him to football every Saturday. Jack idolised him. It would be a shock now for him to learn that his father wasn't the superhero he imagined him to be.

"Your father's a compulsive gambler," Rose said bluntly.

"No, he can't be, not seriously. Sure, he has a little flutter on the horses occasionally, but everyone does that."

"It's not a little flutter." Rose realised she needed to shatter his illusions about his father. She felt bad doing it, but he needed to understand the extent of the problem, for his own sake, as much as hers. Philip was a user. He wouldn't hesitate to use his own son if it helped him to feed his addiction. "He spent every penny we possessed. He remortgaged the house by forging my signature, and he blew the lot, including all our savings."

Had she been naïve and missed the signs? But, like any addict, Philip hid it well. He'd wrapped up the sorry state of their life in a web of lies that she would never be able to unravel.

The truth came as a total shock, and yet, she should have known after twenty-one years of marriage. She should have read him better and realised something was wrong. She should have realised about Sandra Dennison, too.

It had been like wearing a blindfold. She admitted she might have been too comfortable. Something needed to rock them in one direction or another. But when it came, instead of a gentle rocking movement, it turned out to be a massive bloody explosion that destroyed the foundation of her life. Now the shockwaves of the aftermath threatened to destroy their son. She should have seen it coming, but perhaps her subconscious chose not to.

Jack had long since finished eating. In a delayed reaction, he let his knife and fork clatter angrily onto the empty plate. "You should have stopped him. You shouldn't have let him do it."

"I'm sorry, Jack." It wasn't her fault. *Why doesn't he get that it wasn't my fault?* "Your father's an adult. I can't stop him from doing anything.

Besides, he didn't want me to find out, so he hid everything from me. That's what addicts do."

"Dad's not an addict. He made a mistake. You can fix this."

Philip made a massive mistake, shattering everything into a million pieces. Their lives couldn't be superglued back together, even if either of them wanted to try. Rose didn't know how to make Jack understand that. She hoped he would come round when he had more time to process the situation.

"What about your job?" Jack asked. "You should have stayed in Manchester for that."

The waitress put two steaming plates of pasta in front of them, bolognese for Jack and creamy salmon pasta for Rose. She added a liberal amount of black pepper to her fish, while Jack spooned copious amounts of grated Parmesan onto his bolognese.

"I lost my job." She didn't want to elaborate. Let him think what he liked. She absolutely wouldn't admit to him she'd been fired, and she certainly would never tell him why. She needed Jack to respect her, not to label her as a loser. "I've got a job down here."

Jack raised an eyebrow while sucking up a strand of spaghetti.

"I'm managing a shop," she said. It sounded better than the reality.

"Ok." Jack seemed doubtful.

Did he doubt her capabilities? Running the shop so far proved pretty similar to what she'd done in the insurance company. It was all about being organised and dealing with people, so basically the same skill set. The only difference being that the job in the shop required no reference. Thank God for Sarah because, currently, Rose was unemployable. Once anyone applied to her old company for a reference and learned why she'd been fired, she would never get another job.

"Have you spoken to your father in the last few days?" Rose asked, eager to change the subject, although there was no safe subject between them, not today.

"I tried phoning the landline, but it wouldn't connect."

"I'm sorry. I should have told you all this a week ago. It's a shock. I'm still trying to come to terms with it myself." *Not to mention trying to come to terms with all the other crap in my life.* "And I didn't want to tell you the bad news over the phone."

"Dad should have phoned me," Jack said.

"Yes, he should have." At least they agreed on something: Philip was a total shit.

Rose forced herself to eat her pasta, even though she'd suddenly lost all her appetite, despite it tasting delicious. She needed to make herself eat because there wouldn't be much money left to buy more food until she got paid again.

"Gran's flat's got a spare room if you want to come and visit one weekend," Rose said. "It would be lovely to see you."

"What about Dad? Will I be able to visit him too?"

"I expect so, darling, but you'll have to ask him that. I don't know what the arrangements are with his new woman."

"Have you met her? What's she like?"

"She's a bit younger than me." Rose omitted the fact that she was prettier, with a better body and longer legs. None of those things counted for much, not really, did they? Except, right now, they seemed to be the most important things in the world. One more thing she didn't want to admit to Jack, that Sandra used to be Rose's boss.

Sandra Dennison turned out to be a pretty ungracious winner too, yet another thing Rose wouldn't be sharing with Jack. As far as Sandra was concerned, she'd won both prizes, her job and Philip, not that Rose considered Philip to be a prize now. More of a liability, really. Sandra was welcome to have him. She could have him gift-wrapped, if she was foolish enough to take him on.

"Do you want dessert?" she asked Jack.

"I wouldn't mind." Jack pushed his empty plate to one side.

Rose asked for a dessert menu. She was hoping he would say no, but she couldn't deny him. She just about had enough money to pay for it all. At least dessert would prolong her time with Jack, giving her at least an extra twenty minutes with him before she needed to go home, an extra twenty minutes to make sure they parted on good terms, hopefully with Jack understanding that none of the blame for this mess lay with her.

Chapter 10

Rose wanted to be sure Jack was ok before she left him, so it was after ten o'clock by the time she got off the train at Brackford station, later than she'd planned to be. According to the timetable posted in the bus shelter, the bus should arrive within a few minutes. Rose shivered in the chilly night air, hoping the bus would arrive on time before she became too nervous about being out late in the evening. At least there were enough people here to make her feel moderately safe. But this was central Brackford. There would be no crowds of people on the final short walk home.

The double-decker bus was packed, forcing her to sit upstairs. She picked a seat right next to the stairs, away from the group of rowdy young men commandeering the back seat. Rose tried to ignore them and stared out the window instead.

She realised she didn't have a clue how long it would take her to get home or how many stops it might be. She glanced at her watch as if that would make the time pass quicker. Behind her, a scuffle broke out, making her feel very uncomfortable.

"You dare disrespect me, and I'll slit your bloody throat. D'you understand me?" a sharp voice shouted.

Rose tried to ignore them, but the whack of flesh on flesh made her immediately swing round, nervous about keeping her back turned towards the fight.

"What you staring at?" An angry face glared in her direction.

She shrunk back, avoiding eye contact, and turned round again. The violence upset her, stirring up too many memories she was trying to forget. She didn't want any trouble. As soon as the bus reached the next stop, she would go downstairs. Even if the lower deck remained crowded and she had to stand up, it would be safer than staying here. The hairs on the back of her neck bristled with fear. Was Brackford always like this? She supposed she would need to get used to it if she carried on living in Mum's flat, but she wasn't sure if she would cope with staying here long term. A bit of angry banter could easily turn into a fatal stabbing. Some of these boys were wired. Were they on drugs? If they'd taken something, they would be extra volatile. They might turn in a heartbeat. She didn't want to be here when that happened.

Behind her, the fight continued. Still, she didn't dare turn around again. It sounded as if more of them were joining the ruckus. She could just about make out the nucleus of the fight from the reflection in the window. The action edged closer towards her. Rose clutched her fingers around her bag, ready to get up and leave as soon as she got the chance.

"Get off me, you bastard." The boy let out a high-pitched, fearful whine.

The boy's fear transmitted to Rose and, for a moment, she froze, absolutely terrified. Then she got a grip on herself and stood up, tottering dangerously at the top of the stairs as the bus jolted unexpectedly. The sooner she got off this bus, the better. She sensed that something bad would happen if nobody stopped those boys. She couldn't do anything. It would be foolish to try. Perhaps if she alerted the bus driver, he would call the police. There must be protocols for this sort of thing. Anyone driving a bus in this area late in the evening must have come across scenarios like this before.

The bus jerked to a halt, shooting Rose forwards so she tripped down the first couple of steps. She gripped the rail tightly to regain her balance, then hurried down the stairs, keen to find another seat before the bus moved off again. The bus didn't stop for long. Rose had barely descended half the stairs when it pulled away again. She hadn't seen anyone get off. Perhaps the bus only stopped for a traffic light. Rose hung onto the rail grimly while she negotiated the remaining few steps.

The crowd hadn't thinned out much on the lower deck. No way would she be able to push through to the front to report the fight to the driver. Presumably, the bus would be equipped with cameras. The driver might already be aware of the events unfolding upstairs.

Downstairs, it became much more difficult to see anything outside the bus. She had no idea where she was and lacked confidence that she would recognise her stop in the dark.

The shouting upstairs continued. The noises of a serious fight blasted down the stairs to the lower deck. Rose edged her way towards the door, willing the bus to go faster.

"Excuse me." She tried to push past the group of people blocking the bus's exit. Her stop must be coming up soon, but other passengers hemmed her in on all sides, blocking any chance to see outside. The man in front of her finally shuffled over a few inches and she managed to squeeze through the gap. This road appeared vaguely familiar, although everything looked different in the dark. Suddenly, Rose spotted the shop in the distance. The bright lights inside illuminated the doorway and the sign above the door. It made a welcome sight.

Rose stretched to press the button to signal the driver to stop. The bell tinged, shortly followed by the bus slowing to a halt. She pushed her way through the other passengers to the open door. Once off the bus, she quickly got her bearings. The shop lay just beyond the bus stop to her left, with her flat a few minutes' walk to her right.

Rose began walking towards home. Sensing a presence behind her, she swung around to check who it was. The two men must have got off the bus after her. She recognised them from the upper tier of the bus. The one wearing the distinctive brown jacket had been part of the group fighting. Rose told herself not to worry. Both men probably lived around here. Only the size of the two men made them seem threatening, not anything they did. Even so, Rose's gaze automatically fixed on the lights from the shop, with the sanctuary of Alfie's presence. The proximity of the shop compared to her flat made the decision easy. Instinctively, she crossed the road and power-walked towards the shop door. She didn't dare to check behind her, in case it drew attention to her vulnerability. As her hand pushed against the shop door, she caught sight of the two men reflected in the glass. She surreptitiously glanced towards them as she hurried through the doorway. Why were they watching her? She admonished herself for being paranoid. They didn't know anything and certainly not that she'd witnessed Roman's murder. They probably weren't even aware of her run-in with Jordan Taylor. Was she simply an easy target, a woman on her own late in the evening? Perhaps they'd been planning to mug her without making it anything personal. Either way, she was glad to see Alfie.

"Hello, darling. I didn't expect you today. How's that son of yours?"

Rose almost cried with relief. Alfie's cheerful banter immediately made her feel safer. "He's good. I took him to a lovely Italian restaurant."

"Nice. Colchester, isn't it?"

Rose nodded. She glanced up at the clock on the wall. Nearly closing time. Would it be too much of an imposition to ask Alfie to walk her back to her flat when he closed up? She checked him up and down, critically appraising his usefulness as a bodyguard. Could she ask an old man to protect her against two fit young men? It wouldn't matter. Simply the fact that she wouldn't be alone would deter the younger men. They may even have gone home by now. She should stop worrying about nothing.

"I'm about to close up," Alfie said. "Why don't I walk you back to your flat. I'm going that way."

Rose's shoulders relaxed instantly, making her realise how tense she'd been. "That would be lovely." She gave Alfie a big smile.

"No problem. It's not a great place to be walking on your own late at night."

That observation didn't fill Rose with confidence. Lately, she heard more and more rumours about the dangers of living in this locality. She wondered why the police didn't patrol the area more if crime here was really as widespread as people said. But people always embellished the facts of a story, so most likely the rumours were exaggerated.

They walked quickly, Rose eager to get home in case the two men still lurked nearby.

"You don't hang around, do you?" Alfie said.

Rose wondered whether she should admit about the men who may have been following her or the fight on the bus. If she did, Alfie might give her some good survival tips, since he'd lived in this area for a long time. "Sorry." The words came pouring out. She couldn't help herself. "I got a bit spooked by a fight on the bus coming home, and then two men got off the bus behind me. I'm sure they weren't interested in me at all, but I still felt threatened. That's why I came to the shop. I didn't want to walk home on my own."

"Don't worry about it," Alfie said. "You'll be safe with me."

It reassured her, simply having somebody else with her. But the fact remained, Alfie wouldn't be much use against two younger men.

They arrived at the entrance to her block of flats. "This is me," she said. "I'd offer you a drink, but all I've got is tea."

"A cup of tea would be lovely." Alfie smiled at her.

Rose unlocked the communal entrance door. She hoped, as they walked up the stairs, that she wouldn't give Alfie the wrong idea, the idea that he might be getting more than a cup of tea.

"Come in, I'll put the kettle on." She gestured to the small dining table at the end of the kitchen. Alfie pulled out a chair and sat down.

"Your mum used to come in the shop a lot. She spoke about you sometimes."

"Really? I hope she didn't say anything bad." Rose laughed.

"Nah. She was really proud of you. I'm sure she would have liked more regular visits, though. Always making excuses for you, said you were too busy and lived a long way away."

"Yes, we lived in Manchester." Rose hoped he wouldn't quiz her too much on her recent life. She didn't want to talk about Philip and the mess he'd got her into.

"Manchester's not exactly the moon. Couple hundred miles? Just saying."

The kettle clicked off, and Rose poured water into the mugs she'd already set out. She didn't need Alfie criticising her. The guilt was already eating her up. Of course she should have seen Mum more often, but she had wanted to spend her weekends with Philip. Fat lot of good that did her. She might as well have visited Mum. At least then, something good would have come out of the whole mess and her mother would have been happier.

"How long have you lived in this area?" Rose asked, keen to change the subject.

"It's got to be over twenty years," Alfie said. "I moved here when I left the Army."

Rose glanced over at Alfie. Suddenly, she saw him with fresh eyes. He might be better bodyguard material than she'd previously imagined. "I didn't have you down as a soldier. Should I call you Sergeant Major?"

Alfie laughed. "Captain, actually."

Rose did a mock salute at him. "Ok, Captain Alfie."

Alfie sipped his tea. "Anyway, the neighbourhood's gone downhill a lot during that time."

"Are you still happy living here?"

Alfie shrugged. "Got no reason to move."

Rose noted that he didn't completely answer the question. She let it be. "I overheard some men on the bus talking this evening. They mentioned someone called Terry, said he'd done someone in. I wondered if it might be connected to Roman's murder." Rose was rather pleased with the lie. Perhaps she could do something after all to get Terry and his friend convicted, without actually getting involved and putting herself in danger.

"It's possible." Alfie tapped his fingers on the table. "But violence is rife in this area. Whatever you overheard, it might be nothing to do with Roman."

"Do you know anyone called Terry?" Rose watched Alfie's face carefully, looking for any sign that he might be lying.

"I can think of a couple of Terrys around here. It's a common enough name."

Alfie's face didn't give anything away—a proper poker face, but the hesitation before he answered made Rose suspect he was holding something back. "Who are they?" she asked.

"They're not people you want to get involved with," Alfie insisted.

"So I'd like to know who I need to avoid." Rose looked him in the eye, daring him to ignore her request.

"Ok, so there's Terry Carter, and there's Terry Thompson. Are you always this insistent?"

"Yes. So who are they exactly? Tell me something about them. Are either of them likely to be murderers?"

"Well, there's a question. What happened to innocent until proven guilty?"

"I just—"

Alfie interrupted her. "Terry Thompson lives with his mother on the Hale Hill Estate. He seems ok, as far as it's possible to tell, but he's in with the wrong crowd, so who knows."

"And Terry Carter?"

"He's rumoured to be involved with the gangs, but it's just a rumour. The police haven't managed to get anything against him, as far as I'm aware. But there isn't exactly a huge police presence in this area."

"Why not? Surely, they should be patrolling all the time if the area's that bad." Rose wondered how to check out Terry Carter. He seemed by far the most likely candidate of the two Terrys Alfie mentioned.

Alfie laughed. "Reckon they're afraid," he said. "The official line is, they don't want to aggravate the gangs, but the truth is, they're frightened of them. Really, it isn't *that* bad here."

"To be honest," Rose said, "I'm getting a bit worried about walking home late in the evening. I wondered if you wouldn't mind doing the late shift more often." Rose looked at Alfie pleadingly.

Alfie nodded slowly. "I can do most evenings, but I can't do seven days a week. Even I'm not superhuman." He laughed.

"It's only six," Rose said. "We already close early on Sundays."

"That's my wild social life down the pan." Alfie laughed.

"Can we close a bit earlier?" Rose bit her lip. Perhaps she should have considered the pros and cons of the idea more carefully before she suggested it, but she was still trying to work out the best way of asking Alfie for a description of Terry Carter, without him realising what she was planning. Closing earlier would mean working fewer hours, and consequently a drop in earnings. But she didn't want to spend any evening walking home in fear. "If we close at ten instead of eleven, at least we avoid pub chucking out time." That might be a good compromise and wouldn't reduce her earnings by very much.

"Yes, ten's all right with me, but we should run it by Sarah. I worried for a minute you might suggest closing at five." Alfie laughed. "The whole point of these little convenience stores is that people can shop at any time, although honestly at least half the people around here are unemployed, and the other half will mostly go to one of the big supermarkets and they're open pretty much twenty-four-seven these days. We only make money because people are too lazy to travel further."

Rose let out a huge sigh of relief.

"Are you sure you're cut out for working in the shop? You do need to deal with lots of customers, and some of the people around here can be a bit rough. Not what you're used to, I expect."

"I'm fine," Rose insisted. She couldn't afford to lose this job.

"Then you need to toughen up. Stop showing them you're frightened, then they'll respect you."

"Yes, I suppose so. I'll try."

Alfie drained his mug of the last dregs of tea. "I should be going," he said. "How about I work six till eleven tomorrow evening, and we'll put up some big notices saying we're going to change our hours and close at ten p.m. starting next week? I'll discuss it with Sarah, but I'm sure she won't mind. We don't get many customers late at night anyway, and it will save on the electricity bills."

"Thank you," Rose said, "for everything."

As soon as Alfie left, Rose realised she still didn't have a clue what Terry Carter looked like or where to find him. She considered passing on his name to the police but, without evidence, the police would be powerless. She would have to think of something else.

Chapter 11

Rose hurried down the stairs at 7:05 a.m. on Monday morning. She'd overslept, and she was supposed to open the shop at seven. She hoped there wouldn't be a queue outside by the time she arrived, although honestly, the shop was rarely that busy first thing. Someone passed her on the stairs.

"Pardon, did you say something?" She thought he had spoken to her, but she was so wrapped up in worrying about being late that she hadn't been paying attention. She glanced round quickly. A man in a black leather jacket briefly looked at her as if she were an idiot as he continued to walk up the stairs. He pointed at his phone. She hadn't even seen the phone.

"I'll be there in half an hour," the man said into the phone. His voice reminded her of someone, but she couldn't remember who. She ignored it and carried on, eager not to be any later than she already was.

For the first time since she started her job, someone was waiting for her to open up the shop. "I'm so sorry I'm late," Rose apologised.

"Don't worry, love. I only came for some milk." The lady smiled at her.

Rose hoped she wouldn't mind yesterday's milk. Today's fresh delivery wouldn't arrive for another half-hour. She fumbled with the lock, then raced behind the counter to key in the alarm code. The woman went straight to the back of the shop. She'd obviously been in here before. A small shudder raced through Rose as she recalled her own experience when she'd been down that end of the shop, hiding like a coward from Roman's murderers.

Suddenly, she recalled something else. That man on the stairs just now. She remembered where she'd heard that voice before. He was one of them, one of Roman's murderers. She didn't know for certain which one. Was she sure? She racked her brain, trying to remember more clearly. Now she started to doubt herself. It might be him. Or was it simply the local accent that sounded similar?

"You ok, love?" The woman held up a pint of milk in front of her.

Rose snapped out of her thoughts. "Sorry." She scanned the milk bottle and took the money for it. "Will there be anything else?" She always tried to get some extra sales out of people. It's what she'd been taught to do on the phone in her old job at the insurance company in Manchester: dazzle them with your politeness and encourage them to spend more money by upgrading their cover. The strategy didn't work this time. Rose smiled at the woman. "Have a nice day."

At the end of a long day, Rose was pleased to hand over to Alfie.

"You look whacked," he said.

"Thanks," Rose said sarcastically. "I guess I still haven't recovered completely from my late night and all the travelling to visit Jack on Saturday."

"In Colchester? That's not far. I get now why you didn't visit your mum very often from Manchester. That must have felt like travelling halfway around the world to you."

Rose laughed, unsure whether to take him seriously. He'd hit a nerve with that remark about not visiting her mother enough. She still suffered from the guilt. "I'll see you tomorrow," she said, "if I can cope with the journey from my flat." It still felt strange calling it *her* flat. In her head, the flat still belonged to her mother. She should try to make it a little more homely, stamp some of her personality on it, but that would take money, and cash remained extremely tight.

She appreciated being able to walk home in daylight. It was early April, so the evenings would get lighter quickly as summer came. Plenty of signs of summer showed already, with a few early tulips growing in a couple of gardens and some rose bushes already in bud. Most of the front gardens were concreted over for car parking, or they overflowed with rubbish, but every now and again she noticed a garden that received regular loving care. What a pity her flat lacked a garden, although she worked so many hours, she'd never find time to tend it, or enjoy it.

As she got halfway up the stairs, wondering what to cook for supper tonight from her sparse supplies, Tanya opened her door.

"Hi, Tan, how are you?"

Tanya smiled at her. "I was coming down to the shop to ask what time you finished work," she said. "You've saved me the trouble."

"I'm finishing at six now most days."

"Do you fancy coming round for supper? I've hardly seen you since you moved in. It would be nice to get to know you. There's not many people in this block our age. They're mostly pensioners."

Rose immediately cheered up. "That would be lovely." All she had left in the cupboards was a tin of baked beans. Her stomach rumbled, and she realised she'd missed lunch. "What time?"

"Is six thirty ok?"

"Yes. Do you want me to bring anything?"

"Shall we go posh and have a bottle of wine?"

Rose wished she hadn't asked. Now she would have to pop back to the shop and buy a bottle. "Red or white?"

"I like red," Tan said. "It's got more guts to it."

"I'll see you at six thirty. Thank you. I'm looking forward to it."

Rose knocked on Tanya's door at exactly half past six, clutching a bottle of Shiraz that she'd popped back to the shop to buy earlier.

"Come in." Tan gave her a hug and took the bottle of wine.

"Something smells delicious," Rose said.

"It's only a bit of pasta and sauce." Tan led her into the kitchen. "Take a seat."

Tan pulled out a couple of glasses from a cupboard and filled them generously with wine.

Rose hoped she wouldn't be hungover in the morning. Alcohol was the first thing she'd given up on her tight budget, so this would be the first drop she'd touched since the day after moving here. Too much wine would go straight to her head. She took a cautious sip, trying to eke it out until she got some food inside her.

Tanya dished up the meal. The aromas coming from the saucepan as she lifted the lid smelled divine. Tan served the Bolognese sauce with pasta bows instead of spaghetti, with some green beans on the side. Rose hated spaghetti, especially the way it dribbled down her chin whenever she tried to eat it. The bows were a huge improvement.

"This is the best meal I've eaten since I moved in upstairs." It was true. It tasted even better than the Italian meal she'd eaten with Jack. And as for what she cooked herself these days, she'd been living on rubbish, lacking time, money, and the motivation to cook decent food. She resolved to try harder. She could make tasty meals, even on a budget. "What did you put in the sauce?" It was delicious.

"Secret ingredient." Tan winked. "Sun-dried tomato paste. It was on special offer, so I figured I'd give it a try."

"It's lovely."

"How are you enjoying your job in the shop?" Tan asked.

"It's great," Rose said. "The hours are long, but I'm meeting lots of new people, and it pays the bills." *Just about.* "I'm so pleased that I'm able to do something to help Sarah. It must be hard for her losing her husband like that."

"How she's doing?"

"I think she's struggling to come to terms with things, but that's only to be expected." Rose had hardly seen Sarah since she'd started the job. After work tomorrow, she'd pop to the shop flat to check on her. She wished she were able to do more for the family. Perhaps she could. For a start, she should tell the police what she knew about the man called Terry and his accomplice. But she wouldn't. It would be putting herself in too much danger, and it wouldn't help Sarah one bit. The only way to do that would be to find some evidence against Terry, giving the police grounds to actually arrest and charge him. She didn't have much luck finding evidence against Jordan Taylor, and right now she couldn't even identify this Terry for sure. For Jack's sake, as well as her own, she refused to put her safety at risk for nothing. She was certain Sarah wouldn't expect her to, but the guilt still kept her awake at night.

"It's so nice to have a friend nearby," Rose said. Most people around here seemed to keep to themselves. That always seemed to be the way anywhere near London. The people here weren't nearly as friendly as Northerners. She missed Manchester, but it would be difficult to go back, thanks to Philip. She wondered if Philip had spoken to Jack yet. Jack promised to call him after her visit yesterday, but she wasn't convinced that Phillip would be man enough to answer the phone, however much Jack wanted to speak to his dad. She hoped they had made contact by now. Let Philip do some explaining. Why should she take all the flak? Although he'd probably spin things to make himself out to be the big hero and tell Jack everything was her fault instead. She doubted he would admit to his gambling addiction. He refused to even admit that to himself, so he would never confess his failings to his son.

Thinking about Philip made her reach for her wineglass and take a big gulp. She put it back on the table, not wanting to become as bad as him. She must get Philip out of her head before it depressed her any further.

Rose picked up her wineglass again. "Here's to our new lives." She clinked glasses with Tanya. This was a new start for her. Things surely must improve from now on. Once she got her next pay packet, she'd be on top of things financially and could afford to buy decent food and a few other things she'd managed without lately. If she budgeted her money really carefully, she might even be able to afford an occasional fun evening out with Tan.

"How are you getting on with Alfie? I've met him a few times in the evenings."

"He's great," Rose said. "He's been really helpful."

"I'm not sure what to make of him," Tan admitted. "He doesn't give much away. I've chatted to him lots, but I don't know anything about him at all. I suppose we all have secrets."

"I don't know much myself," Rose said. "He used to be in the Army, so he says." She finished her last mouthful of bolognese, wiping her plate clean with a piece of crusty bread.

"I bet he can handle himself well, in a fight, I mean. That might come in handy in this area."

"He's over sixty." Rose wasn't sure Alfie would be any match for a younger man. She hoped she would never need to find out.

Tan got up and started clearing away the plates. "So? He's still in good shape, by the looks of him."

Rose agreed. She was glad Alfie would manage the shop most evenings instead of her.

Chapter 12

The shop was quiet this morning, so Rose spent much of her time tidying shelves and restocking where necessary. As she tidied up the checkout area, she discovered some large sheets of Perspex leaning up against the wall right at the back. Rose wondered what they were used for. They looked quite big, with an arch at one end and some brackets screwed onto them.

Of course, she should have realised. It came to her in an instant now. They must be the screens that had been fitted in front of the till during the Covid epidemic. She searched around the front of the counter and located the spare screw holes where the screens must have been attached. It would make her feel so much more secure if they were refitted. She looked around the shop, wondering what other security measures might be possible. Sarah had already told her the CCTV cameras didn't work anymore. They relied on two big mirrors, strategically positioned so that whoever sat at the till could keep an eye on customers at the far end of the shop. They'd caught a few shoplifters that way, but it provided no deterrent to violence or a serious robbery, and no evidence if anything untoward took place.

Rose decided to mention it when she visited Sarah after she finished work this evening. Maybe they could afford to replace or mend the CCTV cameras. Business was going well, apart from the odd quiet morning. Perhaps people sympathised with Sarah and wanted to support the shop because of Roman, or maybe the locals were simply curious to meet the new girl. Probably the former, and there was no guarantee how long that effect would last.

She would ask Sarah if they might put the screens back up. Alfie would do that for her. Anything that would help her feel safer would be welcome.

The bell above the shop door tinkled as the door opened. Rose looked up to greet her customer. "Good morning," she said cheerfully.

The old man nodded at her. "You're new," he said. "Where's Roman?"

The question took Rose by surprise. No one had asked her that question before. News seemed to travel fast around here, so everybody knew what happened to Roman. She wondered how this man managed to miss the news. The local papers were buzzing with it, and everyone in the neighbourhood still talked about it.

"I'm really sorry. Someone attacked Roman a few days ago. I'm afraid he died."

The man grew pale. "No, that can't be right. Why would anyone want to harm Roman?"

"Have you known Roman long?" Rose asked. She wondered if she should fetch a chair for the man to sit down. He seemed quite old and frail and she didn't want the shock to set off a heart attack.

"I've known him ever since he moved to the area," the man said. "I come in here nearly every day usually, but I've been in hospital since last week."

"That explains why you didn't hear the news. Are you all right?" She didn't want to have to perform first-aid in here for the second time this month.

"Have they had the funeral yet?" the man asked, ignoring her question.

"No, not yet," Rose told him. "His wife is still organising that."

"What happened? How did Roman die?"

Rose wasn't sure what to say. Of course she wouldn't admit she'd been in the shop when the murder took place. "Someone stabbed him, but the police haven't caught the person responsible yet. Sadly, he died on the way to hospital." Talking about it hadn't helped her. It brought back memories that she'd been trying to forget, despite trying to remain calm and matter-of-fact about it. She would definitely talk to Sarah about security later.

She hurried to the storeroom out the back of the shop, reluctant to leave the shop unattended even for a few seconds, but needing to fetch a chair for the old man. She didn't want him collapsing on the floor.

The old man introduced himself as Clint, and he lived on the same road as she did. He'd even known her mother. They used to go to some pensioners' club together on a Thursday afternoon. Once he recovered from the shock of hearing about Roman, he became quite chatty.

"You seem to know everyone around here," Rose said.

"Lived here my whole life, and I'm seventy-six next month," Clint said proudly.

Rose smiled at him. "Have you ever met someone called Terry Carter?" Rose tried to sound casual, but inside, her heart pounded violently against her chest.

"Little weasel, he is, always has been. I used to work with his dad at one of Devlin's warehouses. I gather he's working for the same company now."

"Can you describe him?" Rose asked.

"Ginger hair. At least, it was ginger last time I saw him, but that was ages ago, and young people are always dyeing their hair, aren't they? Me, I prefer to stick to my natural colour." He pointed to his thinning silver-grey hair. "What you see is what you get."

The bell above the shop door tinkled, signalling the arrival of another customer. To Rose's relief, Clint got up and said he needed to get home. She'd been afraid that he would start quizzing her about her interest in Terry Carter.

Rose realised Clint hadn't actually bought anything. She thought about reminding him but decided he'd probably only come in for some company. She guessed she would soon see him again.

Immediately after Rose finished work, she went upstairs to the flat above the shop to find Sarah.

"Come in. I'm just helping the children with their homework."

Rose was pleased that Sarah seemed to be coping better. "Have you organised the funeral yet? If there's anything I can do, you only need to ask."

"It's going to be on Tuesday afternoon," Sarah said. "I'm dreading it. I'm not sure how I'm going to survive it."

"No one's expecting you to be perfect. Everyone will be there to support you. What's going to happen with the shop, for the funeral, I mean? Do you want me to keep it open, or should we close it as a mark of respect, just for a couple of hours?"

"I hadn't even thought of that," Sarah said. "Would you like to come to the funeral? You were there when..." She didn't need to finish the sentence.

"I'll do whatever you want me to do. It would be nice to come, but I'm happy to keep the shop open if you prefer." The last thing Rose needed was another funeral, but perhaps it would help give her some closure. "I assume Alfie will want to attend the funeral."

"Perhaps it would be better to close the shop for the afternoon. I'm sure some of Roman's regular customers will want to pay their respects, so I expect the shop won't be busy then. It does seem disrespectful to carry on, regardless. I wish I knew what Roman would want me to do."

"I'm sure he would want you to do whatever you feel most comfortable with," Rose said. She wished she hadn't started this conversation. How could she steer it onto the subject of security? And, if she did, would it remind Sarah of that awful day of her husband's murder?

"Is everything all right in the shop? Are you happy?"

Rose decided she may as well speak her mind. Whatever she said, it would be impossible to make Sarah feel any worse than she already did. "I love the job," Rose said. "But I found some Perspex screens, the ones everyone used when Covid was at its peak. I wondered if it might be a good idea to put them back up, just to give a bit more protection.

I'm sure what happened to Roman will never happen again. He was so dreadfully unlucky. But better to be on the safe side, don't you think?"

Sarah considered for a few seconds. "Yes, of course you should put the screens up if that makes you safer. I'd hate for what happened to Roman to happen to anyone else."

"Thank you," Rose said.

"I'm sure Alfie can fit them for you."

"I'll ask him. Also, can we spare enough money to buy a couple of CCTV cameras? You know the existing ones are broken. It would be a good deterrent, and if the worst does ever happen, we've got evidence. We have been very busy lately, so there should be enough money to pay for it." Rose had absolutely no idea how much new cameras would cost, or how much money they'd made this week. Had Sarah got to grips with the shop's accounts yet? Rose guessed that Roman previously did everything, and Sarah wouldn't even have looked at it yet.

"I haven't really thought about money yet." Sarah confirmed Rose's suspicions. "I wouldn't know where to start."

Rose didn't hesitate. "I can help you with that. I've done a little bookkeeping." To say she'd done a little bookkeeping might be exaggerating. She'd done a minuscule, microscopic amount. But mostly, bookkeeping simply meant adding up lists of things, working out how much you spent on different items, and counting the cash in the till, and the bank. Easy stuff, which only required a bit of common sense and a calculator. She got the impression she'd be much better at it than Sarah. She worried that, if she left the business side of things to Sarah, the shop might end up bankrupt before anyone even realised. Someone needed to take charge.

"Are you sure? You're doing enough already. It's just that Roman used to do all that, so I really don't have any experience." Sarah glanced over at her children, clearly wanting to turn her attention back to them.

"Of course I'm sure. And I can probably fit in most of it between customers while I'm working, so you won't need to worry about it taking up any extra time." It would be much better if she knew exactly how much profit the shop made. If she saw signs of the business falling to pieces without Roman running it, it would be preferable to have plenty of warning, in case she needed to find another job. But that wouldn't happen. She wouldn't let the shop fail.

Chapter 13

To Rose's surprise, when she got home, she found Philip sitting outside her block of flats.

"What are you doing here?" Rose regarded her husband with suspicion. Since she'd moved here, she'd had trouble even getting him to answer his phone, yet now he had shown up in person. Had Sandra thrown him out already? Well, she wouldn't let him stay with her, that's for sure. He'd well and truly burned that bridge.

Philip smiled. "It's lovely to see you too, Rose."

"I suppose you'd better come in." Rose guessed he wanted something. She steeled herself not to cave in and give it to him. If he needed money, he'd be disappointed.

Rose pointed Philip towards a chair in the kitchen and filled the kettle. "What do you want, Philip? You obviously didn't drive all this way for a social call."

"Coffee, two sugars, please."

Rose glared at him in disbelief. "I do remember how you like it. Too bad I don't have any coffee. You can have tea, or you can go home. Take your pick." Rose found it hard to believe that only recently she still held out hope of her and Philip saving their marriage. But after what he did to her, gambling away the family home and all of their savings, she couldn't even look at him anymore without wanting to punch his face. What did Dorothy tell her? *Love flies out the window when the bailiffs walk in the door*. That definitely proved true in this case, what with Philip recklessly destroying their security. She used to believe in their marriage. She'd believed in him. If they'd lost all their money under different circumstances, she would actually have stuck by him because she'd loved him. But Philip's actions destroyed that love.

"I've brought you a present," he said.

Rose laughed bitterly. "What is it, a kite?" She poured two mugs of tea.

Philip looked puzzled. "What?"

"A kite. With strings attached."

"Ah." Philip didn't deny it.

"So what do you want?"

Philip hesitated.

"I haven't got any sugar." Rose plonked one of the mugs on the table in front of him, putting it down so angrily that some of the hot liquid slopped onto the table. She reached for a cloth. "I'm sure your so-called gift won't be anything I want." She wiped up the mess and slung the cloth in the sink.

"You'll want this," Philip said.

Rose held out her hand. "Where is it then?" she asked cynically.

"I left it in the car," Philip said.

At least he hadn't lost the car yet, but it was only a matter of time. Technically, the car half belonged to her. She should make him sell it and give her half the money, except he probably owed a lot of debt on it. The car would be worthless by the time the loan company took back its share of the sales proceeds.

Philip got up. "Come down to the car with me. I'll need some help to carry it up the stairs."

Rose followed him. She would escort him back to the car, then tell him to shove off. That would be the easiest thing to do. Then at least he would be out of her flat.

She locked her door and followed him down the communal staircase. "Have you spoken to Jack?"

"Not really," Philip said.

Rose resisted her overwhelming urge to push him down the stairs. "Don't you think you owe it to him to explain what happened? The truth, not the rose-tinted, fairy tale version."

"Ok. I'll phone him. Tomorrow."

It was always *tomorrow* with Philip.

Philip had parked his car on the road opposite the flat. He unlocked it, gesturing her to examine the contents laid across the back seat.

Philip's car was packed with Rose's jewellery-making equipment. She reached out, stroking her toolbox, her tubs full of supplies, metals and semiprecious stones, and her workbench folded up beneath all the boxes. A huge smile lit up her face. Immediately, she tried to suppress it, not wanting to give Philip the upper hand by showing her delight.

"Where did you get it? You told me the bailiffs took everything." This was amazing. If she could supplement her income by making a few pieces of jewellery in her spare time, it would help her get back on her feet quicker. More than that, she loved designing jewellery. She'd missed that creative outlet.

"I wouldn't let them take this," Philip said. "I told them it belonged to you, and they couldn't have it. Nearly got myself beaten up over it."

"You kept it all this time and didn't tell me?" How could he do that? Rose wondered if he'd planned to sell it, no doubt imagining it would fetch a lot of money, but it wouldn't have been easy to sell. It was a specialist market for the equipment, and the gemstones were mostly garnet, not rubies or emeralds.

"What's important is I've got it now."

Rose reached out to take a box.

Philip put a hand on her arm, stopping her, and thrust an envelope in front of her. "You can have everything as soon as you sign this," he said. "I'll even carry it up the stairs for you."

Rose tore open the envelope. Inside was a divorce petition. She dropped the document as if it might burn a hole in her hand, then bent down to pick it up, taking her time in order to compose herself before having to face Philip. Even though she hated Philip now and had finally lost any desire to save their marriage, this still came as a shock. Or perhaps the blatant rejection was what upset her more.

"You haven't wasted any time, have you? Why the big hurry?"

Philip said nothing.

Suddenly, Rose got it. "Oh my God. You want to marry Sandra, don't you?"

Philip nodded. "Are you going to sign it?"

Rose couldn't wait to sign Philip out of her life. "I'll need to read it. You should make a start with carrying some of this lot upstairs." She gestured at her equipment.

Philip picked up a token box and locked the car. "Come on then."

By the time Philip carried all of her equipment upstairs, Rose had read the entire document. Without paying a solicitor to check it over, it looked ok to her. Luckily, there were no assets left to share out or young children to get caught up in custody battles. Everything should be simple. She took a pen and signed. She understood why Philip wanted to move on quickly. It would only be a matter of time before Sandra discovered his gambling problem and the state of his finances, then she would probably kick him out, leaving him homeless. Perhaps Sandra really did love him. No, Rose knew Sandra Denison better than that. The only person Sandra truly loved was herself. Well, she was very welcome to Philip. They deserved each other.

Chapter 14

Wednesday arrived all too quickly. Rose had counted out one hundred pounds the afternoon before and put it somewhere safe. She wanted to make sure Alfie didn't deposit it in the bank, leaving her with insufficient cash. Now that cash burned a hole in her pocket, while she waited for the men to show up to collect it.

Rose's nerves jangled more than ever today. They had buried Roman yesterday. It should have given her some closure, enabled her to move on, but the thought of those men visiting every week loomed over her like a dark cloud of fear. She tried to forget about them. Luckily, a stream of customers kept her busy so, for a while, she managed to ignore her worries completely.

She had just taken delivery of some frozen foods when a man she didn't recognise came in. Immediately, her nerves returned. Her hand flew straight to her pocket, fingering the cash to check it was still there.

"I'm looking for someone called Rose," the man said.

Rose didn't connect the red hair instantly. After her previous experience, her suspicion grew, especially given his unfriendly attitude. "Who wants to know?" She needed to get these frozen items in the freezer before they started to defrost. The box of ice cream would deteriorate quickly at room temperature. But that was the least of her worries right now.

"Terry Carter." He looked at her intently. "Are you Rose?"

Rose should have guessed from the hair colour. But she never expected Terry Carter to show up asking for her. What had Clint been saying about their conversation? She dropped the box of ice cream into the freezer without unwrapping it while she decided what to say.

"Why have you been asking about me?" Terry gave her an angry stare.

Rose considered denying everything, but Terry was already convinced of her identity. She wished she could hide behind her Perspex screen right now. He scared her, and she wondered if it was true what they said about redheads having tempers. This redhead certainly seemed keen to prove the theory correct.

"I found a credit card with your name on it on the floor," she said, improvising quickly. "It must have been dropped on Wednesday a couple of weeks ago. Were you in here that day?" Would he admit to being in the shop on the day of Roman's murder? It was worth a try.

"Where is it then?" Terry held his hand out.

"Where is what?"

"The credit card." Terry looked at Rose as if she were a complete idiot.

Rose inched away from him. He made her feel uncomfortable. She'd expected him to say it wasn't his, that he hadn't lost his credit card. Maybe he had several cards and wouldn't notice if one went missing, or maybe he was just chancing his arm and would take someone else's credit card if it was offered to him. "I don't have it anymore." How was she going to explain this? Rose wished another customer would come in. "I handed it in at the police station. It seemed like the best thing to do." She banked on him not wanting to go anywhere near the police, like most people around here. "I'm sure they'll let you have it if you go to Brackford police station."

"Nah. Can't be mine anyway. I was at work that Wednesday. Worked overtime too, so I never would have come over here."

Rose smiled with relief that her story hadn't been a complete failure, although it was annoying that Terry seemed to have an alibi. She cast her mind back to that dreadful Wednesday, trying to remember what the voices of those two men sounded like. She couldn't say for sure whether either of them might be Terry Carter. They all spoke with the local accent. Everyone sounded similar to her. One thing was for sure. Neither of the men who visited her earlier was Terry Carter. She seemed even further away now from finding out who killed Roman Marek.

After that, Rose remained surprisingly calm when the two men showed up asking for their protection money. Rose handed it over without speaking. The entire transaction was over in a couple of minutes. She breathed a massive sigh of relief when they left the shop, although she kicked herself for not asking their names. If she knew their identities, perhaps she might pluck up the courage to report them to the police. Neither of them was Terry Carter, that much was certain, but that didn't mean he hadn't been involved with Roman's murder.

She remembered Clint mentioning the name of the company Terry Carter worked for, Devlins. As soon as Rose found herself alone in the shop a bit later, she looked up a phone number for Devlins, dialling it before she changed her mind.

"Hello, this is PC Katherine Perry from Brackford police," Rose said. She put on her most officious telephone voice, hoping her ploy would work. "I need to confirm if one of your employees was at work on Wednesday the week before last. Terry Carter."

"Let me check for you."

Rose held her breath while she waited, cringing at the awful canned music. It seemed to take forever before the woman came back on the line.

"Hello. Yes, Mr Carter was here from nine a.m. until nine p.m. that day."

"Thank you for your help." Rose ended the call. Hopefully, no one would ever trace it back to her. She wondered what the penalty would be for impersonating a police officer.

She looked at her watch. Alfie would be here soon to take over for the evening shift. Sarah had invited her to supper this evening and, although Rose didn't think it was the best idea, with the funeral only being yesterday, she understood when Sarah explained she didn't want to be on her own.

"How's my favourite lady now?"

Rose had been so deep in thought she didn't even notice Alfie come in. "You're early."

"Only five minutes."

"Well, I'm glad you're not late. I've got a dinner engagement," Rose said.

"Oh really? A gentlemen friend, is it?"

Rose wondered if Alfie was jealous. Probably not. She flattered herself. She pointed up at the ceiling. Alfie looked puzzled. "Sarah and the girls."

Alfie raised his eyebrows in surprise, then smiled again. "Lucky you, Sarah's a good cook."

"I'd better go." Rose didn't want to be late, then she would be able to leave earlier. She didn't relish the idea of walking home on her own, not after the events of today, but if she timed it right, perhaps Alfie would walk her home.

"Come in." Sarah welcomed her with a hug. "Thank you for coming. I hope I'm doing the right thing. I just wanted some normality for the girls. It's been a difficult day. I thought perhaps a distraction..."

Rose nodded. "Of course." She was glad Sarah looked a little happier than earlier, as if the funeral had lifted a huge weight from her, although Rose guessed some of Sarah's demeanour might be put on for her benefit.

"Come and see our pictures." Olivia, Sarah's older daughter, ran to greet Rose.

"Livvy, sweetheart, give Rose a chance to take her coat off first," Sarah said.

Rose handed Sarah her thin raincoat, which she held draped across her arm, not bothering to put it on just to walk upstairs. "Lead the way, then. Show me your works of art."

Chloe, Olivia's younger sister, sat at the kitchen table colouring in her picture with crayons.

"Can I see?" Rose moved closer to examine the drawing.

Chloe snatched up the piece of paper, holding it to her chest. "Not finished yet," she said.

"Mine's finished," Olivia said proudly. She held the picture out towards Rose.

Rose took it carefully and turned it towards her. The artwork showed some promise. The dog in the picture looked like a cross between Snoopy and an orange Labrador. Yes, it lacked a little realism but did vaguely resemble a dog, and the shading gave it the texture of fur. For an average nine-year-old, this was probably as good as it got.

"That's brilliant. I love the shaggy fur. Has it got a name?"

"His name's Brian," she said as seriously as only a nine-year-old could when talking about an orange dog.

"Hello, Brian." Rose smiled. She wished Jack were still this age, when life had been so simple. She started to make the comparison that Olivia's life was simple too, like any nine-year-old. But she wasn't just any nine-year-old. Nothing simple about a nine-year-old with a murdered father. Nothing to be envious about.

Rose handed the picture back to Olivia. "You're a very clever girl," she said. She turned back to Chloe. "Have you finished your picture yet? Can I see?"

Chloe carefully placed her red crayon on the table. She held the picture out shyly, not saying anything.

Rose took it carefully, worried that Chloe would snatch it back and tear it. For a moment, she wondered what the picture depicted before realising it was upside down. She turned it around, realising it must be a person, and a car, or at least, a six-year-old's interpretation. She examined it more closely. Yes, definitely a man in the car, of sorts. The man was lying down. And the car? Green and yellow. Rose puzzled over it for a few moments, then a lightbulb came on in her brain. Of course, those were ambulance colours. Chloe had shaded in the man with red crayon, making his entire body a mass of bright red scribble, like blood.

Rose looked away, blinking back the tears that threatened to flood out. How could a six-year-old child depict in such graphic detail the tragedy that had befallen her father? Rose found it disturbing. She wondered if Sarah had seen the picture yet. Chloe clearly needed some help to process events. The school would be able to find them a child psychologist. Half of her wanted to pick up Chloe and hug her, and the other half wanted to burst into tears and run away. *Stop it, Rose*, she told herself. She couldn't keep running away from everything. Like earlier this afternoon, when she'd briefly considered quitting her job in the shop and leaving Sarah in the lurch. Had she seriously contemplated doing that? She looked at Chloe and her heart broke. She wouldn't be leaving anytime soon.

"Supper's nearly ready," Sarah said. "Girls, put your drawings away, please, and lay the table."

"Can I help with anything?" Rose hated to let Sarah do it all.

"Absolutely not. You sit down," Sarah insisted. "You're a guest, and you've been working hard all day. It's good for the girls to learn to help." She lowered her voice to a whisper. "It will take their mind off things."

Sarah produced a delicious casserole with homemade dumplings. "It's a traditional Polish dish," she explained. "Roman's mother gave me the recipe a few years ago."

"It's lovely. Thank you so much for inviting me." Rose didn't eat much home cooking these days. By the time she finished work, she was usually knackered, and she didn't have enough money to buy decent food, anyway, not until she'd paid off her credit card balance. She should make more effort, but making tasty food out of cheap ingredients took so much longer, and she would rather put her feet up in front of the TV and relax in the evenings.

"It's my pleasure," Sarah said. "I wanted to thank you for everything you've done for me, managing the shop. I'd be lost without you."

Rose blushed. "It helped me too. I really needed a job." She would never tell Sarah how desperately, never admit that she'd been fired for hitting a colleague, even though that colleague stole her husband, and then provoked her about it. Would anyone really blame Rose for reacting, for lashing out like that? Basically, the incident made her unemployable. Her old employer would never give her a reference, not one worth having anyway. She needed to remember that fact the next time she contemplated packing in this job. She was lucky to have any job at all.

Anyway, Sarah had enough on her plate, what with grieving for her husband and looking after a disturbed six-year-old child. She didn't need the worry of losing the shop's main employee. Most of all, Rose refused to let the lowlife who killed Roman win. She renewed her determination to stay.

As soon as they finished eating, Olivia and Chloe wanted her to play games with them. "Nothing too energetic," she warned them. "I've eaten too much to run around."

They seemed happy, at least on the surface, and Rose enjoyed being part of a family again, even if only for a couple of hours. Chloe seemed to have forgotten about her drawing and ran around giggling like a normal six-year-old should. Maybe the drawing acted as her therapy. Depicting the scenes that ran through her head might be helping her to process events and move on. Life was never that simple, but perhaps for a six-year-old, it might be. Rose wished she understood what Chloe was going through.

"Right, time for bed," Sarah called to the girls.

"Oh, Mummy, do we have to?" Chloe looked pleadingly at Sarah.

Sarah picked her up. "It's past your bedtime, young lady. You're tired."

"I'm not tired," Olivia piped up.

"It's still past your bedtime." Sarah put Chloe down. "Go and get ready for bed, girls. I'll come and tuck you in soon."

"I should be going home." Rose didn't want to get in the way of Sarah putting her children to bed.

"Please stay," Sarah said. "It would be so nice to have a grown-up evening, even for an hour or so. I bought a nice bottle of wine specially."

Rose didn't take much convincing, and it beat going home to an empty flat. "That would be lovely." If she timed it right, she would ask Alfie to walk her home.

Chapter 15

In another half-hour, he would be here. Rose had been looking forward all week to Jack's visit. He promised to stay the whole weekend. She spent all her free time this week tidying up the flat, trying to give it a more homely appearance, and clearing out the spare room to make it nice for him. Rose missed her son. It would be wonderful to see him. She'd spoken to him several times on the phone since that meal in Colchester. Thankfully, he'd forgiven her after he'd spoken to his father, who Jack told her sounded like a total wally, running around after some younger woman.

Rose hoped Jack wouldn't be too disparaging about the flat. It wasn't what he'd been used to in Manchester. It might be a small flat in a less than salubrious area and in desperate need of modernisation, but it was *hers*. At least she could provide Jack with somewhere to live if he needed it, more than his father was prepared to do at the moment. She shouldn't be so worried. As a student, Jack must be used to slumming it by now, living in cheap digs. This wouldn't be nearly as bad. Rose tried her hardest, blowing much of her budget for the month on some decent food and a nice bottle of wine. She would live on bread and water for the next couple of weeks if she needed to, or even go to the food bank, which she had resisted so far because she didn't want to rely on charity. Her pride wouldn't let her accept it. The food bank would be her absolute last resort.

"Are you ready?" Sarah called from the shop doorway. Sarah had kindly offered to drive Rose to the station to collect Jack.

"Just coming." Rose said goodbye to Alfie. Jack texted her five minutes ago. He would arrive at the station soon.

"Thank you for doing this," Rose said to Sarah as she shut the car door and pulled on her seat belt. "I'm worried he might not find his way here on the bus." After her last experience of taking the bus home from Brackford, to be honest, Rose worried much more about Jack's safety on public transport than she did about him getting lost.

"Really, it's no trouble." Sarah headed the car towards Brackford. It wouldn't take long to get to the station.

"Who's looking after the girls?"

"They're having a sleepover with some friends, so I get a bit of peace and quiet and a chance to catch up with the housework. I might just manage to finish tidying up by the time they get back and start making a mess again." Sarah laughed.

They neared the station. "Look, there he is," Rose said excitedly, pointing at Jack standing outside the station, carrying a big holdall.

"I can pull up next to him if he's really quick getting in. There's room in the back for his bag."

Jack slung his bag onto the back seat before jumping in after it. Sarah pulled away before she got into trouble for parking in a no waiting zone.

Rose twisted in her seat to see Jack properly, longing to hug him, but that would have to wait until they got home. "Jack, this is my friend, Sarah. Sarah, this is my baby boy, Jack."

"Mum," Jack protested. He always hated it when she called him her baby boy. "I'm an adult now."

Rose ignored the protest. "It's so good to see you."

The journey home went even faster than the drive to the station. "Do you remember Gran's flat?" Rose asked. "When did you last visit?"

Jack stayed silent, and Rose imagined him sitting behind her, shrugging.

"The last time must be about five years ago," she said. They stopped visiting as a family. Rose visited her mother on her own after that, leaving father and son to do some male bonding in her absence, which usually involved going to a football match. "It was Easter. Mum bought you a huge Easter egg. Do you remember?" She wondered how much Jack would recollect of her mother's home. They would soon find out.

Sarah pulled up outside the block of flats.

"Do you want to come in?" Rose felt obliged to ask, especially as Sarah didn't have the children this evening.

Sarah politely declined, to Rose's relief, as she really wanted Jack to herself. Rose thanked her once again for providing the transport.

"Thanks, Sarah," Jack said, climbing out of the car.

Rose rushed to help with his bag. She tried to gauge his reaction as she led him up the three flights of stairs to the flat.

Tanya opened her front door as they approached. Rose introduced Jack proudly, wondering if Tan was watching out for them, just to be nosy.

"Lovely to meet you," Tan said. "Listen, Darren will be home this evening. How about we all four go out to the local pub for a pint? It will be nice for the two men to have someone their own age to talk to."

"That would be great," Jack said.

He'd accepted before Rose got the chance to voice her opinion. She really wanted to keep Jack all to herself, but she was being selfish. Of course Jack would rather talk to someone his own age. And if he made a friend here, perhaps he would visit her more often.

"See ya later." Tan hurried down the stairs.

Rose unlocked the door to the flat. At least it would be just herself and Jack for a couple of hours. "Pop your bag in the bedroom. It's first on the right." Should she have given up her bedroom for him and slept in the spare room herself? She'd pondered that question for hours yesterday, deciding in the end that it would be a lot of disruption moving all her stuff. Now she doubted the decision. The pretty pink rose-covered wallpaper in the spare room and pink-flowered duvet on the bed weren't suitable for Jack. Her mother had kept the room for her, for the few occasions she bothered to visit. Rose resolved to redecorate it soon with something more masculine.

"Shall I make you a cup of tea?"

"Have you got any Coke?"

Rose hadn't. She'd forgotten Jack's love of Coca-Cola. "I can pop out to the shop and get some."

"Don't worry, Mum. A glass of water will do fine."

Rose hurried to fetch it. She should get dinner on, especially as they didn't have so much time now before they needed to go to the pub. She planned to make chilli con carne. He'd always loved that, and it was a bonus that it used cheap ingredients, so she wouldn't blow her budget yet.

"Is the room ok?" she asked when he came back.

"It's fine, Mum. Don't fuss." Jack parked himself at the kitchen table, slouching with his elbows in front of him.

Rose began chopping onions, then put some rice on to boil. "How's university?"

Jack shrugged. "Yeah, good, thanks."

"What sort of things are you doing on your course?" She hoped Jack wouldn't give her one-syllable answers all evening. It would be nice to have a proper conversation with him. Tears came to her eyes. It must be chopping the onions that made her want to cry.

"Oh, a load of boring stuff. But also, I'm learning judo, and I'm training the local under twelve's football team." Suddenly, Jack became animated and interested in the conversation.

"That's exciting," Rose said. Jack always loved sport. His teachers tried to push him into something more academic. Seeing him now, Rose was thankful he'd stuck to his guns and followed his passion.

"There's a lad on the team. I reckon he might be the next David Beckham."

"Really? How wonderful." Rose remembered wanting to be the next Posh Spice, but the next David Beckham sounded pretty good.

"Yes, you should watch the way he controls the ball. He's very talented. With the right coaching, he's going all the way."

Rose hoped that Jack would be that coach, that his star pupil wouldn't be plucked from under his nose to be trained by someone more experienced, the most likely scenario if the boy really possessed as much talent as Jack made out.

"Shall we give the local pub a try?" Tan suggested. "I've not been there yet."

"I suppose it's difficult with you working nights." Rose opened the pub door. The Thief and Beggar didn't sound like the most upmarket name for a pub, and from her experience of the area so far, Rose's expectations were low.

"If it's got beer, it'll be ok." Jack followed her inside.

"I'll drink to that, mate." Darren came right behind him, leaving Tan to bring up the rear.

"What's everyone drinking?" Rose felt obliged to offer, even though she still constantly worried about spending too much money. Tan had cooked her dinner this week, not to mention being very generous with cups of tea and biscuits. At least this place didn't look expensive.

"It's a rough place," Jack said when they were all sat down with their drinks, "but at least it's within easy walking distance."

Rose took a sip of her gin and tonic. "I wonder why it's called The Thief and Beggar."

"It certainly describes a few of the people living around here," Tan said.

"Well, let's hope this is the nearest any of us ever get to begging." Jack laughed.

"Mum says you play a lot of football," Darren said to Jack. "Which team do you support?"

"Man United, of course. We used to live in Manchester, but I'd support them anyway because they're the best team in the world."

"They're rubbish," Darren said. "Surely Manchester City is the best team in Manchester, although Arsenal is much better than both of them."

"In your dreams." Jack made a face at Darren.

Tan laughed. "I think these two might need a referee soon. Let's not start a riot over it. It's only football."

Darren glared at her. He looked up again and smiled, then stood up and waved at someone across the room. "Ash. Over here," he called out.

Rose snapped her head around to see who Darren was shouting at. To her horror, one of the men who had asked for protection money from the shop approached their table.

"Ash, this is my mum." Darren pointed at Tan, who smiled sweetly at the man. "And these are Jack and Rose, our new neighbours."

Ash sat next to Darren. Rose didn't know what to say. Ash definitely recognised her. She didn't want to make a fuss in front of Tan and Darren, but she also didn't want to spend the rest of the evening with this man. She would certainly struggle to be nice to him.

"Nice to meet you," Ash said. "Does anyone need a drink?"

Rose needed a drink. If she had to spend the next couple of hours being polite to Ash, she would probably need a full bottle.

"Two beers and two G 'n Ts, please," Tan said without hesitating.

Ash didn't seem to mind and headed straight to the bar.

"How do you know Ash?" Rose asked Darren.

Darren shrugged, reminding Rose of Jack. "We went to the same school."

Ash expertly attracted the bar staff's attention, putting Rose's earlier efforts to shame. He soon returned with a tray of drinks and five bags of crisps.

"Thanks, mate." Darren grabbed the cheese and onion crisps before anyone else got the chance.

"So, what do you do, Ash?" Rose stared at him, whilst still trying to be casual.

Ash didn't blink. "I'm a businessman," he said. "And what do you do, Rose?"

"Rose runs the local shop," Tan said.

"Yes," Rose said, "although it seems to be very difficult to make enough money to live on."

"Perhaps Ash can give you some business advice," Tan said. "He makes loads of money, don't you, Ash?"

"I do ok," he said. "I'd be happy to give you the benefit of my experience." He smiled at Rose. "I'll come into the shop next week."

"No rush," Rose said, fighting the urge to throw her drink over him.

Rose wondered how she would manage to make polite conversation for the rest of the evening. Tan wasn't helping matters one bit. She needn't have worried. The boys soon started talking about football.

Ash only stayed for one drink. Rose was relieved when he left. Would he keep coming to the shop demanding protection money after learning of her friendship with Tan? She doubted he possessed a conscience or any kind of loyalty. In any case, he probably didn't get any choice. He would have to do whatever the gang leaders told him to or suffer the consequences, making it highly unlikely that anything would change for Rose.

Chapter 16

Rose walked home quickly from the shop at lunchtime on Saturday, smiling all the way. Alfie insisted on covering for her this afternoon and the whole of tomorrow, to enable her to spend the time with Jack. She would heat up some soup for lunch, and she'd bought some nice crusty bread to go with it. Would that be enough for a fit young man who played a lot of sport? Already, she worried that things might not be good enough for Jack. She desperately wanted him to enjoy this visit.

"I'm home," she called as soon as she opened the door.

"In here." Jack sat watching TV. "Man United's playing," he said. "It's a replay of the match I missed yesterday. It finishes in ten minutes."

The whole family supported Manchester United football team, even Rose, who didn't like football. Supporting Man U was practically compulsory in the area they'd lived in, not too far from the football ground. Rose wouldn't get any sense out of Jack until the match finished. Ten minutes would be just enough time to fix lunch.

Ten minutes later, Jack joined her in the kitchen as she poured leek and potato soup into bowls. She put the bread on the table with some butter.

"I thought we might go and put some flowers on your gran's grave this afternoon." Rose blew on her soup, which was far too hot to eat. "It will give us both the chance to explore the area." It would also make a cheap activity for them to do together, and she didn't think her fitness-freak son would baulk at walking for half an hour. She felt bad that she wasn't able to take him somewhere more exciting, but Jack had regretted missing her mother's funeral, and it would do him good to visit her grave.

"Sure." He tucked into his soup, immune to its hot temperature, dipping chunky pieces of bread into it and wolfing them down.

Rose bought a bunch of carnations yesterday and put them in a jam-jar on the kitchen windowsill. Seeing them now, they didn't seem adequate. Mum deserved better, but that wouldn't happen until her money situation improved.

The route to the crematorium cut through a scrappy area of the council estate, peppered with tired-looking blocks of prefab concrete flats, and footways littered with rubbish and potholes. She should have found a nice shortcut through a park instead, but if the local scenery disappointed Jack, he hid it well.

It was a relief when they arrived.

"Where's Gran?" Jack asked.

Rose had momentarily forgotten about Jack not attending the funeral. He'd needed to attend a vital lecture from some visiting sports personality, who Rose had never heard of, but Jack seemed terribly impressed by. Rose insisted he didn't come to the funeral. She desperately wanted Jack to do well in his degree, get a good career, be the best, make the most of all the advantages she'd missed out on at his age. It was the right decision. No regrets. But without Philip either, she was the only family member to turn up at the funeral.

She surveyed the area, trying to get her bearings, struggling to remember the exact location of Mum's grave, too ashamed to admit she hadn't visited even once since the funeral.

"I'm not sure. Maybe I used another entrance before. Everything looks different from this direction." Rose hoped there were two entrances to the graveyard, so that Jack wouldn't find her out.

"No worries. We can walk around them all. What colour is her headstone?"

"She hasn't got one yet," Rose said. "You can't erect a headstone for several months. The ground has to settle first." Rose found it a huge relief to learn that. Her mother's headstone was yet another expense she needed to save for.

"Makes sense." Jack started walking around the perimeter of the graveyard.

Rose quickened her pace, trying to keep up with Jack's long legs, whilst scanning the graves for one that looked familiar, one without a headstone.

It didn't take long to locate Mum's grave. A small wooden cross with her name on it served as a temporary marker until she got a proper headstone. Rose took the jar from her carrier bag. She filled it with water and screwed the lid on tightly before they came out. Now she arranged the meagre bunch of flowers she was clutching and set the jar of flowers on the grave. A bunch of tulips in a cheap but pretty vase already adorned the space. Who brought them? A lot of people attended the funeral, friends of her mum, many of them old people. It might be any one of them. It was nice of them to care, although it made Rose feel even more guilty. Iris was *her* mother. She should have put flowers on her grave before now.

Jack looked around, clearly bored.

"Shall we try to find a different route home?" Rose suggested.

"If you want."

Rose got the impression that Jack would rather be at home watching football for the rest of the afternoon. She'd been on her feet all morning in the shop, so she'd also be quite pleased to relax for a while. Since she didn't actually know any alternative routes home without getting lost, she opted to retrace their steps.

The walk home seemed quicker, probably because Jack upped the pace. They soon reached the flat.

"Cup of tea?" Rose offered as soon as they got inside.

"Thanks, Mum."

"How long are you planning to stay here?" Jack tapped his fingers on the kitchen table in some sort of musical rhythm that Rose didn't recognise.

Rose hadn't really thought about it. "I don't have any plans to move at the moment."

"Won't you go back to Manchester?" Jack's eyes pleaded with her.

"I don't have any plans," Rose said, trying to think of even one good reason to go back. If she was honest, she wanted to be as far away as possible from Philip, to avoid any chance of bumping into him or the traitorous Sandra. She hoped Jack didn't assume that she and Philip might get back together one day. Kids always wanted that, didn't they? She reminded herself Jack was no longer a kid, but that wouldn't stop him from hoping for his parents to reunite.

"I don't like it here," Jack said. "It's a rough area. I'll worry about you when I'm in Colchester."

"It's really not that bad. Yes, it's a poor area. Everything is a bit shabby. But I wouldn't call it rough. There are some nice people living here." Rose shut up before he accused her of protesting too much. Jack's assessment was spot-on, and he didn't know the half of it. She thought it best not to tell Jack about Roman's murder or about Jordan Taylor. He would definitely worry if he found out about that. Rose hadn't even told him that his gran was murdered, glossing over the details when he'd asked. Truthfully, she didn't have much choice unless she sold the flat and moved somewhere else. She doubted the flat would be worth enough to fund moving to a nicer area. And there was the employment problem to consider. She hadn't mentioned that to Jack either, losing her job in Manchester, her lack of a reference, her unemployability.

"It looks rough to me."

"Don't worry, I'll be ok." Rose hoped it wouldn't put Jack off coming to stay during his university holidays.

"Mum, you've got no idea how to handle yourself. Let me teach you some self-defence moves. I've learnt a lot in my martial arts training."

"I'm fine. I can't see myself giving someone a karate chop in the street. I'm not Superwoman."

Jack laughed. "It's not like that. There are little things you can do if anyone ever attacks you. Things that even old people can do to protect themselves."

"Are you calling me old?" Once Rose got on the wrong side of forty, her age quickly became a sensitive subject. Time was passing her by. For all she'd accomplished so far in her life, she may as well be a hundred years old. She looked at Jack proudly. He was probably the only really good thing she'd achieved so far.

"Course not. But will you let me show you some stuff? Please, Mum."

Rose hesitated.

"It would help with my training, to have some practice at teaching the moves."

"Ok." Rose gave in. She followed Jack into the living room, where he pushed the sofa back to give them more space.

"You're not going to throw me on the floor, are you?"

"Mum, will you just trust me?"

Rose hoped this wouldn't get too energetic. She wished she hadn't drunk that cup of tea.

Jack stood in front of her. "Grab my arm."

Rose took hold of his arm, holding it gently.

"No, harder than that. Hold it like you don't want me to escape."

Rose did as he asked. She'd never been strong. Her idea of a death grip probably felt like a fly landing on his arm.

"That's better. Now watch me carefully." Jack deftly twisted his arm, releasing it from her grasp instantly.

"Now I'm going to grab you and I want you to do the same thing and free yourself."

"I can't. You're much stronger than me." This was a waste of time.

"Can you at least try, please? Remember, you need to twist your arm to escape my grip," Jack said calmly.

Rose started to twist her arm. Jack had matured a lot since he'd been away at uni. The old Jack would have lost patience by now and stormed off in a huff. His grip on her arm seemed tighter. She brought her elbow up and rotated her arm quickly. Immediately, Jack lost his grip on her.

"Did you let me win?" She simply didn't believe she'd released herself from Jack's hold. He was so much bigger and stronger than her. How could that be possible?

Jack shook his head. "No. I promise, I tried to hold on. Do you want to run through that again?"

They practiced the move twice more and Rose gained in confidence. Perhaps this would be useful one day, although she hoped she'd never have to put the knowledge into practice.

"That's great," Jack said. "Let me show you another move." He stood in front of her again, pointing to his throat. "If you want to really disable someone, punch them or just flick them right here."

Rose laughed. "I don't understand how that's going to hurt anyone." A big manly punch might work, but a little flick, which was probably all she could manage, would do nothing.

"Mum, why don't you trust me?"

"I do trust you, but—"

"But what?" He didn't wait for an answer. "I didn't want to have to do this, but I guess I'll have to prove to you it works. Go on, flick me in the throat."

"Ok." Jack would go on all afternoon about it if she didn't. At least it would prove to him that she was incapable of doing anyone any damage. Rose reached up to his throat and flicked her finger into it, deliberately not trying to do it too hard because, for once, she wanted to be right.

Jack grasped his throat and fell to his knees, wheezing and coughing and fighting to catch his breath.

"Are you ok?" He struggled to breathe. Rose knelt down beside him, fraught with anxiety, unsure what to do. Why was he reacting like this? Did he have something wrong with him that he was keeping from her? She patted him on the back in case he was choking. Why couldn't he breathe? "Jack?" She got up to search for her phone. Jack needed an ambulance, but they would never get here in time.

Jack erupted in a coughing fit. He put his hand up, waving it at her. Rose didn't quite understand what he meant by the gesture. She felt so helpless.

Suddenly, Jack seemed to improve. He took some deep breaths, gasping in air.

"Now," he rasped, still trying to inhale. "Now, do you believe me?" He forced the words out with difficulty.

"Are you ok, Jack?"

He nodded, still breathing heavily.

The relief nearly overwhelmed Rose. She knelt down and draped her arm around him. "I'm so sorry," she said. "Are you sure you're all right?"

Jack got to his feet and sank into an armchair. "I'm fine." His breathing was almost back to normal now. "Do you believe me now? You are perfectly capable of disabling a grown man."

Rose shook her head. "I never would have imagined I could do that. I tried to be gentle, so I didn't hurt you." She'd been so worried. She'd been on the verge of phoning for an ambulance.

Jack smiled. "The agony was worth it. You're never going to forget that, are you?"

"Definitely not." Rose would probably have nightmares about it, her darling boy nearly choking to death. She wasn't sure if she had it within her to inflict that on anyone else ever again, but she wouldn't tell Jack that.

"That's enough self-defence for one day," she said. Her nerves couldn't take any more, and she wanted to be sure Jack fully recovered from his ordeal. "Why don't you put your feet up and watch football, and I'll make you a nice cup of tea."

"Thanks, Mum."

"There's a good film on TV tonight," Rose said, sitting down beside Jack. "We can watch that and order a pizza if you like." Rose had racked her brains to come up with something they might do together that wouldn't cost too much. She still didn't want to admit to Jack about her money problems. He had enough to worry about with exams coming up soon. It wasn't fair to him to pile on extra anxiety when he should be concentrating on his studies.

"Can we do that another time please, Mum? Darren's invited me to a party tonight in Brackford. I'd really like to go. It would be nice to make some friends around here if I'm going to visit often."

Rose forced a smile. "That's ok. You don't want to spend an evening with an old fuddy-duddy like me."

"Mum, I never accused you of being a fuddy-duddy. You're young and trendy for a mum."

Rose knew that *trendy* wasn't the best word to describe her, but she appreciated the compliment. "Do you still want pizza before you go out?"

"Yes, please, Mum. I'm not going out until eight."

Rose smiled, a more genuine one this time. At least she would get some time with Jack, then perhaps she would get an early night. She would give him her spare key so he could let himself in later.

It was still pitch-black outside when Rose woke. She checked the alarm clock on the bedside table: 4:10. She doubted she would get back to sleep now. Served her right for going to bed so early. She rolled out of bed and searched for her slippers, heading for the bathroom. Jack's bedroom door was open. She peered inside the room. The light from the hall illuminated his empty bed. She moved closer. The bed showed no sign of being slept in. Was Jack still at the party? She wanted to phone him to check, but that would probably embarrass him. She should stop worrying. When he was away at university, he must frequently be out

partying all night. She never worried about him then, not when she
didn't know. He was probably having a good time, and she didn't want
to ruin that, but she couldn't help being concerned. She tried to reassure herself that Darren would take care of him and forced herself to go
back to bed.

Sleep didn't come. Rose tossed and turned in bed, constantly anticipating the sound of the front door opening and Jack rolling in. At six
o'clock, she got up. This was her normal getting up time. For a moment,
she worried about work, then remembered she'd taken the day off.

She double-checked Jack's room before going to the kitchen to put
the kettle on. He should be home by now. All sorts of scenarios raced
through her head. Could he have split from Darren and been unable to
get the bus back in the middle of the night, or got on the wrong bus,
not knowing exactly where to go? Or had something far worse happened to him? A picture of Roman, lying on the shop floor haemor-
rhaging blood, flashed into her head. She tried to suppress the image.
Jack was sensible enough to stay out of trouble, and he knew all those
self-defence moves. Rose remembered how easily she had disabled him
for several minutes with one tiny flick of her finger, and a knot formed
in her stomach. She sat down and took a few deep breaths. Was this
what happened after witnessing a murder? Would it constantly haunt
her, giving her anxiety attacks every time anything went wrong?

At 9:00 a.m., Jack's key finally clicked in the front door lock. Rose ran
into the hallway.

"Where have you been? I was worried." That was an understate-
ment. She'd been scared stiff.

"It's cool, Mum. The party carried on late, so Darren and I went
home with his friend and stayed over. I slept on the sofa."

"I wish you'd phoned to tell me."

"I didn't want to wake you up." Jack sat down. "Got any breakfast?"

Rose put some bread in the toaster and poured some tea. Jack looked tired as if he hadn't got much sleep at all.

"Where was the party?"

Jack shrugged his shoulders. "Don't know. Some old warehouse down by the river. Darren's friend's cousin owns it, something like that. It was awesome. There's a monument next to it, a statue of some famous local woman. At the end of the party, they set off fireworks from the top of the statue."

That didn't sound to Rose as if it would be officially permitted, but she said nothing. It might be interesting one day to visit the monument. She enjoyed discovering local history.

Jack smiled at her. Rose always found it difficult to be cross with him for long. He'd learnt as a tiny baby how to wrap her around his little finger, and he'd been doing it ever since. One smile, and it tugged at her heartstrings. She would do anything for him, perhaps because he was an only child. Years ago, she had longed for another baby. She and Philip fought over it constantly for ages, with Philip reluctant to go through all the sleepless nights that a baby entailed. He didn't even click with Jack until his second birthday. Finally, they experienced that father and son moment over a toy car. When Jack got old enough for Philip to take him to watch football, they bonded properly. That must have been where Jack got his love of football and sport in general. They'd spent many hours together watching football, rugby, and cricket on TV. Philip was a watcher, not a doer, so Rose was relieved when Jack turned out to be rather more energetic. But Philip gave up his armchair seat to stand on the sidelines on cold winter mornings to watch Jack play. Was Phillip still proud of his son, or was he simply hoping he might become a Premier League footballer, so he could place a bet on him?

Rose loved having Jack to stay for the weekend, and it came as an enormous relief that he seemed to have forgiven her for leaving his father. She still wasn't sure what story Philip told Jack, but he couldn't have said anything too bad. Maybe she'd never find out. She didn't dare broach the subject for fear of starting an argument and spoiling the weekend.

Sarah phoned to say she was waiting outside to drive them to the station.

"Are you ready, Jack?"

Jack grabbed his bag.

Rose gave him a hug, knowing that she wouldn't get the chance when they dropped him off at the station. "It's been so nice having you here. You will come again, won't you?" She didn't want to let him go.

"Of course I will."

Darren came out of Tanya's flat as they walked down the stairs.

"Hi," Jack greeted them. "I'm glad I bumped into you. I had a great time last night, and please thank Ash for letting me sleep on his sofa."

"Anytime, mate," Darren said.

"You stayed at Ash's house last night?" Rose asked when they were in Sarah's car.

"Yes, he held the party, so he took us back to his place after. It was a great night."

If Jack made friends here, he would be more likely to visit, but Rose was extremely concerned about him having anything to do with Ash. Next time Jack visited, she would have to tell him about Ash and the protection money. She could never risk her son getting involved with anything like that.

The road outside the station was busy when Sarah pulled up, so Jack jumped out of the car quickly.

"Have a safe journey home," Rose said. "Phone me when you arrive."

"Stop stressing, Mum."

Rose waved at him as Sarah drove away, but he was already walking into the station. She would worry now until he phoned. Jack didn't like her fussing, but that's what mums did. She wouldn't be a good mum if she didn't worry about him.

During the short drive home, Rose considered several times bringing up the subject of the protection money with Sarah, but each time she went to open her mouth, she stopped herself. Sarah was doing a good job of holding things together for the girls. She didn't need reminding of the reason Roman died.

Chapter 17

Rose's lovely weekend with Jack made it tough to go back to work on Monday morning. This morning turned out to be much busier than usual, with no time to stop. Finally, she sat down for five minutes to eat her sandwich before the lunchtime rush started. She took a glug from her water bottle, washing down her half-eaten cheese and pickle sandwich. The shop was doing good business recently. Perhaps people were over the initial shock of Roman's murder. In a trade-off between potentially being stabbed or having to walk an extra mile, most of the people around here were lazy enough or incapacitated enough to choose the former option. Especially when the odds of anything happening to them remained pretty low. Indeed, it was equally likely they would get stabbed in the street while they walked the extra mile to the supermarket.

The busy morning really made Rose appreciate a quiet five minutes. She took another bite of her sandwich. At least she didn't have to worry now about Sarah affording her wages. Rose now did most of the bookkeeping for the shop, and takings were well up compared to when she started working here.

The bell above the door startled her. She should have got used to it by now, but she was lost in her thoughts. She hurriedly swallowed her mouthful of sandwich and wrapped up the remains to finish later.

"Good morning." She added a big smile to her greeting. Being friendly cost nothing, and it made the customers come back. Perhaps that explained the improvement in their profits.

As soon as she turned to face the customers, she regretted being so friendly. She froze as she realised it was the brutes who usually came to collect the protection money. They shouldn't be here, not today, on a Monday. They weren't due until Wednesday.

Ash lagged behind the man wearing his usual black leather jacket as if he didn't want to come too close. Did that mean he hadn't confessed to his friend about meeting her in the pub last week? Rose wondered if she should say something. It might get him into trouble. Or it might get him replaced by someone worse.

What were they doing here two days early? Rose supposed she should give them the benefit of the doubt. They may be here to do some shopping. She wished they would choose somewhere else.

"What can I get you?" Her smile was forced now, as if someone had injected her with a massive overdose of Botox, setting her features permanently in position.

The man in the leather jacket smiled back. His smile looked even less sincere than hers. "We're here about the money," he said, staring at her.

"It's not due until Wednesday," Rose said firmly. Best to remain business-like. Don't show any fear.

The man smiled again, showing a full set of teeth that looked ready to eat her. "You're absolutely right. We're here to discuss the increase."

"What increase? We can't afford an increase. There is nothing to discuss. We made an agreement." Rose's heart pounded noisily, and she started to ooze sweat. She hoped the two men wouldn't smell her fear.

"You're absolutely right again." His inane grin made Rose nauseous. "There's nothing to discuss. We want two hundred pounds every week, starting this Wednesday."

"But that's double. You can't double the fee with only two days' notice. That's not fair."

"We can do what we like. We'll see you Wednesday, usual time." He grinned again.

That grin would give her nightmares. She wanted to run after him and slam the door on his arm as he left. They shouldn't be allowed to get away with this. She'd put up with it while they demanded a smaller amount of money, but if she meekly paid up this new amount, they might keep putting the price up, simply because they could.

She looked over at Ash. Immediately, he turned away and she realised that, whatever she said to him, he wouldn't do anything for her. She felt helpless. What choice did she have, except to hand over whatever money they asked for? They'd made it painfully clear who was in control of the situation now.

Rose took a few deep breaths. Her half-eaten sandwich sitting next to her reminded her they had interrupted her lunch, but she'd completely lost her appetite. Was there really no way to stop these men? She worried about it for the rest of the day.

Chapter 18

The man in the black leather jacket headed straight towards the woods. Darkness was falling quickly and Eastbury Park was at last deserted of dog walkers and teenagers taking shortcuts home. Terry should be here by now. He texted him an hour ago, giving him time to get here, but not enough time to go shooting his mouth off about who he might be meeting or where. He walked a hundred yards into the woods and took a left turn. The smell of smoke and the faint glow of a cigarette end gave away Terry's position. The boss was right. Terry Thompson wasn't up to doing this job. No brains, no balls, and you needed plenty of both living in this rough area.

"Tez," he spoke softly, not wanting to draw attention to them in case anyone still lurked nearby.

Terry turned around. The man put his hand to his mouth in a shushing gesture. He didn't want Terry shouting his name.

Terry threw his cigarette on the ground. The man immediately stamped on it. "Be careful," he said. "You'll set fire to the woods." It hadn't rained for two weeks. Bone dry leaves crackled underfoot as if proving the point.

"Sorry."

"How are you, Tez?" he asked.

"I'm fed up with all this hiding," Terry said. "Are the police on to us? Have you found out anything?"

Fear flashed in Terry's eyes. Fear meant mistakes and mistakes meant panic. "Best you keep your head down for a while longer, kid."

"So they are on to us?"

The man patted the pocket of his leather jacket, checking the contents were still safely inside. There was no *us*. This one was all on Terry. Even though it hadn't been Terry's fault, nor was it Terry who wielded the knife that killed Roman Marek, Terry was the one panicking, not him. No way did he want to take the rap if Terry made a stupid mistake and let something slip to the wrong person.

"I'll take care of it," he reassured Terry. "Meantime, we're here to do a job."

Terry said nothing. The whites of his eyes shone out like beacons in the dusk, emanating fear.

"You don't have to do anything much. Just keep a lookout. Can you do that?"

Terry nodded.

The man ushered him towards an enormous oak tree. The massive gnarled trunk encroached halfway across the path, although the branches got regularly trimmed to ensure the path remained easily passable. "Look around the side of the tree. See that track going down the hill?" He pointed, keeping one hand firmly on Terry's shoulder.

"Got it," Terry said.

"I need you to watch the track for anyone approaching. If you see anyone, raise your right hand in the air. Otherwise, don't take your eyes off that track, not even for a second. Can you do that?"

"Ok." Terry leaned against the tree, peeking out from behind it to stare at the track.

The man patted him on the shoulder. "Good lad. Don't let me down."

"I won't." Terry seemed to be calmer now that he had something to focus on.

The man walked five paces in the other direction and turned around. He acted swiftly, pulling on a pair of gloves before opening up his leather jacket and extracting a small handgun from the inside pocket. He aimed and pulled the trigger. It was all over in a second. Terry's body barely had time to hit the ground before the man reached it. The bullet hole in the back of his head delivered instant death.

This wasn't the first time he'd carried out a gang execution for the boss. He liked Terry. He didn't want to hurt him, but when the boss gave an order, it didn't do to argue, not if he wanted to survive. He needed to stop Terry from grassing, whether accidentally or on purpose, and this was the most humane way of doing it. Terry wouldn't have known a thing about it.

He hurried to perform his normal clean-up operation. Taking a small plastic bag from the pocket in his jeans, he emptied the contents of Terry's pockets into the bag, remembering to switch off the lad's phone and remove the sim card, placing the latter in his own pocket. He turned the body over. The bullet had gone right through his head. He used the torch on his phone to examine the tree trunk, immediately locating the bullet embedded in the bark. He gouged it out with a penknife and put it in his pocket, along with Terry's sim card.

The plastic bag containing Terry's phone, his wallet, a packet of cigarettes and a lighter would need disposing of. He took out the wallet, removing forty pounds' worth of notes. Then, in a change to his normal routine, he pulled out the cigarettes and lighter. He lit a cigarette, getting it burning before carefully using it to set light to a heap of dried leaves. If the fire caught, it would burn most of the evidence before anyone noticed it and called the fire brigade.

Finally, he pulled his hoodie over his head and ran along the edge of the woods. He wouldn't use the main exit. He knew a place where it was easy to scramble over the fence. Once out on the road, he turned back towards the woods. The night drifted towards pitch blackness. He sniffed the air, the smell of smoke filling his lungs. Once the fire got a hold, it would spread rapidly through the dry vegetation.

He had three jobs to do on his way home. First, he left the plastic bag containing Terry's possessions in a wheelie bin at the side of the road that awaited the morning collection, burying it under some of the contents. He took the sim card out of his own phone. Tomorrow, he would replace the burner phone he used to contact Terry. He left the redundant phone in another wheelie bin in the next road. Further on, he cut through the footpath towards the river. He broke the two sim cards in half, tossing the four pieces into the river, leaving a few seconds interval between each one, then he took out a second bag, putting the gun inside with some stones to weigh it down, and tossed that into the middle of the river. The gun wasn't traceable to him, but now that it had been used, he needed to get rid of it. Finally, he dropped the spent bullet into the flowing water below.

Silently, he offered up a small prayer for Terry Thompson before walking the rest of the way home.

Chapter 19

Detective Inspector Paul Waterford rolled over in bed, wanting to ignore his phone. He reached for it sleepily, hoping he hadn't woken Clarke, his wife.

"Yeah." He got out of bed and tiptoed to the bathroom, hoping Clarke wouldn't hear him.

"Guv, we've got a body." Paul recognised Kevin Farrier's voice. That was all he needed, being woken at 3:00 a.m., then having to spend the early hours of the morning with that idiot. Now that Paul had been promoted to detective inspector, he should work on getting Farrier transferred out of CID, maybe to the traffic division.

"Where?" Paul rarely felt talkative early in the morning. At this hour, Farrier should count himself lucky to get one-word answers out of him.

"Eastbury Park, guv. The woods at the far end caught fire. Body's pretty badly burned."

Paul groaned. It would be difficult to identify the body, and the smell of burning flesh before breakfast would probably put him off bacon butties for a long time. "I'll meet you there in twenty minutes. Have you called SOCO?" There might not be much for the scene of crime officer to work with if the fire had burned too fiercely.

"Not yet, guv."

Paul crept back into the bedroom to find some clothes. Clarke sat up in bed. "Sorry to wake you, love. Work. I need to go in."

"It's ok. One of the drawbacks of being a police officer's wife, I guess."

Paul pulled on his jeans and hunted for a clean shirt. "*One* of the drawbacks? Are there others?"

Clarke laughed. She seemed more wide awake than him. "Would you like a list? There are plenty of drawbacks. Lucky for you, I love you."

Paul pulled on a thick blue jumper. It would be cold at this time of night. "I just wish I didn't have to deal with Kevin Farrier at this time in the morning." He sniffed loudly. "Not sure I want to deal with him at any time."

"He's not that bad," Clarke said.

"Maybe I can get him transferred to the traffic division."

Clarke swung her long legs out of bed and came over to him, wrapping her arms around his torso. "If you want to get promoted to DCI in a few years' time, you'll need to prove you can manage your team," she said. She let go of him and sat back on the bed.

Paul leaned over and gave her a peck on the cheek. "Try to get back to sleep. I'll call you later." He would think about what she said. Annoyingly, Clarke was usually right, and he did harbour ambitions to continue his rise up through the ranks in the police force. Perhaps he should try harder with Kevin. Perhaps he might eventually manage to turn him into a decent detective.

The fire brigade was still hard at work when Paul arrived at Eastbury Park. The acrid smell of stale wood smoke hung in the air, making Paul cough. Several firefighters hosed down the charred remnants of the fire, causing the hot ashes to hiss as they belched out plumes of steam and smoke. Paul waved as he recognised the station manager, Blue, and headed over to talk to him. All the firefighters went by nicknames. His obsession with the colour gave Blue his nickname. Paul didn't even remember his real name.

"We're nearly done," Blue said. "I don't want to risk the fire reigniting, given it's so close to a residential area. We're lucky the wind isn't blowing in the other direction or the fire might have spread to the houses behind the park."

"Any idea how it started?" Paul asked. Clarke would be sorry she'd missed Blue. Clarke and he were old friends from several years ago, when Clarke had been a firefighter, and she and Blue used to work together.

"Too early to tell." Blue wiped a gloved hand across his face, but instead of removing the dirty smudge across his cheek, he made it worse. "We'll get the Fire Investigation Team out as soon as it's daylight. Can we get the park shut for the morning? We don't want the public trampling over everything until we've finished our investigations."

Paul nodded. Even in the bracing cold night air, his tiredness beckoned him to go straight home and back to bed. "Did you move the body?"

"Didn't touch him. He was well gone by the time we found him." Blue made a face. "It's not a pretty sight."

"Is it ever?" Paul rubbed his hands together. The cold air at this time of night cut through his jumper. He should have worn a coat. Ironically, if he'd got here earlier when the fire was blazing, he wouldn't have any problem with the cold.

Blue sent Paul in the direction of the body. It was situated some way into the woods. Detective Constable Farrier had already cordoned off the area with police tape and stood waiting at the edge of the crime scene.

"What have we got?" Paul pulled on some plastic overshoes, so as not to contaminate any evidence, although the area was pretty thoroughly trampled already by the looks of things, and any remaining traces of evidence were likely destroyed by the fire.

"Looks like a man," Farrier said. "But he's badly burned. He's had a pretty good drenching too."

Paul shone his torch on the corpse. The body was that badly burned, he couldn't determine for certain whether it was a man or a woman, but the general size of the corpse suggested a man. It would be hell to identify him. Perhaps that was the intention.

If they were to find any evidence here, they would need to wait until daylight, which was a good couple of hours away yet.

"It might be best if you stay here until the crime scene gets cleared." It was a lousy job to palm off on anyone, even Kevin Farrier, but Paul had better things to do, like finding some breakfast and a warm coat, and checking out the MOs of local arsonists.

Paul drove to the police station, calling in at a twenty-four-hour McDonald's on the way. There must be some perks to getting up this early, and an egg McMuffin was his current go-to treat, a tasty, unhealthy reward to compensate for the lack of sleep.

It bothered Paul that the park was supposed to be locked at nights, so how did the man get in? Could he be a rough sleeper? Homelessness was a big problem in the Brackford area, particularly since the local hostel closed recently for a major refurbishment.

He fired up his computer and started a list of tasks for the team to get working on as soon as they arrived this morning. He resolved to find Kevin Farrier an important task. Maybe he would get him to attend the autopsy. It would be a good learning experience for him.

Paul really needed the scene of crime report, but it would be hours before he got that. The fire investigator's report might shed more light on the situation, perhaps indicating for certain either murder or a tragic accident. Meanwhile, they should find out about possible missing persons and check CCTV in the area. But the fire investigator's findings might totally change the direction of the investigation. In either case, they would need to identify the victim. Perhaps Kevin could help with that, too.

Eastbury Park stretched along the edge of the notorious Murder Mile area. That suggested the possibility of the death being gang-related. Paul really hoped not.

Chapter 20

Rose got up extra early. She'd started jogging on some days before work, encouraged by Jack to get fitter. She did a lot of walking at the moment anyway, simply to save the bus fare, so running made a logical progression. Three mornings a week before work, she ran to Eastbury Park, doing a lap or two of the park if she got time.

As she approached the park this morning, the smell of smoke irritated her lungs, making her cough. Unusually at this time, the main gates were closed, and beyond the gate, a flurry of activity grabbed her attention. She caught sight of the woods further up the hill. A desolate charcoal scene replaced the vibrant green of early summer. When did the trees get burned? She saw no smoke rising up from them, so the fire must have been fully extinguished already. Had it happened overnight? The blackened trees had really taken a hit from the flames. Overnight, a fire wouldn't be spotted quickly, which would explain the extent of the damage. She reached the entrance and tried to open the gate. It was locked. Perhaps the woods weren't safe enough for the public yet.

Rose paused by the gate, staring up at the devastation and wondering what might have caused the fire. What a dreadful shame. Not only were the trees magnificent at this time of year, but the woods were carpeted with bluebells. They must all be destroyed now.

A police car approached the gates from inside the park and the driver got out. Rose immediately recognised Detective Constable Farrier, which reminded her she never got round to informing him of her return to the area.

"Hello," she called.

Farrier approached the gate. "What are you doing here?"

Rose moved closer. "I'm out for a run. I meant to tell you. I had to come back. I'm living in Mum's flat."

"How long are you here for this time?"

Rose sighed under her breath. "It might be permanent." She was becoming resigned to that fact now and, slowly, it began to feel like a less dreadful fate.

DC Farrier looked concerned. "It's lucky Taylor's still in custody. He's on remand until the trial, but you still need to be careful. He's got friends. If he finds out you're back, he may send them to find you."

Rose didn't want to talk about Jordan Taylor, the man who'd murdered her mother. He'd tried to kill her, too. "What's going on here?" Rose asked, changing the subject and pointing towards the woods. "Why are the gates locked?"

"The woods caught fire last night," Farrier said. "Some poor geezer burned to death."

Rose took a step back. She didn't expect that. "That's terrible. Poor man. Do you know who he is?"

Farrier shook his head. "Going to be difficult to identify him with the state he's in."

Rose shuddered. The image running through her head brought back too many bad memories, of her mother's death and of Rose's subsequent run-in with Jordan Taylor. She had first encountered Taylor in those same woods.

"The park should be accessible to the public by tomorrow," Farrier said. He opened the gates, got back in the car, and drove through.

"Taylor's got a red-hot lawyer. You should go back to Manchester." Farrier locked the gates behind him and got into his car, without a word of goodbye.

Rose watched him drive off. How easy for him to say that, but returning to live in Manchester wasn't an option anymore. She hoped that Taylor's lawyer didn't get him off because she might be well and truly stuck here for the foreseeable future.

Paul didn't expect Blue to phone him so soon.

"What have you got?" Paul asked. It would be a huge help to find out what caused the fire.

"The fire was started by a cigarette," Blue said. He sounded really tired.

Paul wondered if he had been to bed yet. If he'd been on shift last night, he should have finished at 8:00 a.m. He probably hadn't slept yet. "So was it an accident?"

"I didn't say that. It may have been someone trying to make it look like an accident."

"Really?" Paul guessed they should be looking for a smoker. If they were trying to identify a homeless man, that didn't narrow it down much.

Blue went on. "Normally, if it's an accident, the cigarette would be burned right down, and the stub would have been dropped on the ground and smouldered, until it set light to the vegetation."

"But this wasn't normal?" Paul reminded himself he needed to check out any local arsonists. No one immediately sprang to mind.

"No," Blue said. "The cigarette was hardly burned at all. It would never have been discarded like that. It's more likely it got used to set light to something."

"But wouldn't it have burned more during the fire?" Paul didn't understand what Blue was getting at.

"Well, there's the thing. It looks like someone tossed it aside. The fire spread in one direction, but the cigarette got sheltered from the blaze when it fell into a hole. So it didn't burn any further."

"Can we get any DNA off of it?" That would make life much easier. It might identify the arsonist, or the victim, assuming they weren't one and the same person.

"It's possible," Blue said. "We've bagged it up, so you can try."

"Thanks. You should get home to bed. You sound knackered."

"I couldn't sleep, so I came back in. I wanted to make sure this got done."

"Thanks, mate, but really, go home." Paul hoped Blue didn't have to work tomorrow. It was no fun to have to push yourself when you were dog-tired. That's when people made mistakes.

Chapter 21

Rose didn't sleep well on Tuesday night, dreading the return of those men. Worst of all, she'd finally dozed off in the small hours, only to wake with a start at 4:00 a.m., realising she should have asked Alfie to leave enough cash in the till. He always bagged up the takings to put in the bank's night deposit safe on his way home at the end of each day. He usually only left a fifty-pound float in the till, just enough change for them to function. Leaving large amounts of cash overnight would be asking for a break-in.

Rose much preferred it when people paid by credit card, but in this area, people did a lot of cash deals, working for a few extra quid and not wanting to pay tax on it, or, more likely, get their benefits taken away. If the men came back in the morning, and most of her early customers today chose to pay by card, then no way would Rose have enough money to pay them. Not that she wanted to. She still considered taking a stand, refusing to pay the extra. It was extortion. She ought to go to the police, but she got the impression they would be completely disinterested. So far, they hadn't put a lot of effort into finding out who murdered Roman, so why would they bust a gut to track down people asking for protection money. And even if they did, more extortionists would simply spring up in their place.

The shop grew busier throughout the morning, but as Rose feared, most people paid by credit card. Rose guessed they didn't have the money. What size debts were people clocking up on their credit cards that they could never afford to pay? She'd be hard pushed to find even one hundred pounds cash in the till, which was the amount she should really be paying, the amount they'd originally agreed on. She considered phoning Alfie, but although he paid money into the bank, he wasn't authorised to take any out, not without going through Sarah, and Rose didn't want to frighten her with this.

The men probably wouldn't show up until later. Criminals didn't get up early, did they? There was certainly no sign of them yet. It would serve them right if they came too soon.

Clint came in at his usual time of eleven thirty. Rose had quickly grown to look forward to him visiting every day. He lived alone and just wanted someone to talk to and she was happy to oblige in the shop's less busy periods. Often, he didn't even buy anything. Rose hoped today he would break the habit and spend a couple of hundred pounds. She laughed to herself. Fat chance of that. She'd be lucky if he spent a couple of quid.

"How are you this morning?" she said cheerfully.

"All the better for seeing you, my dear," Clint said. "I need a pint of milk."

Rose pointed him in the right direction, completely unnecessary, since Clint knew his way around the shop almost as well as she did.

"You know this area well, don't you?" she said as she took Clint's payment.

"Lived here all my life."

"Do you know of a statue? It's near the river," Rose said. "Some famous local woman." Rose had been meaning to ask him for ages, out of curiosity to find out where Jack had been to that party when he'd stayed for the weekend. She was even more keen to know now. The warehouse next to the statue was owned by some relative of Ash's. It might give her some connection to Ash, some way of finding out his full identity.

Clint put his shopping bag down. "That sounds like the memorial to Agatha Lee. She used to live around here. She saved twenty-one women when the area got bombed during World War II. Led them all to safety, real local hero, she was."

"She sounds like a very brave woman," Rose said.

"Maybe." Clint gave a wry smile. "Some people say she only did it to look after her business interests. Rumour had it that she ran a brothel and all the women she saved were working girls. At one time, someone started a petition to force the council to remove the statue. It didn't get anywhere. The local council's got more important things to do with its time."

Clint sounded as if he might talk for hours on the subject if she gave him the chance. "Where is the memorial?" Rose asked, cutting him short.

"It's at the end of Lee Road. She even got a road named after her. If you want to see it, there's a footpath down to the river at the back of the cemetery."

"Yes, I'll go next time I get a day off," Rose said, wondering when she would find the time.

As soon as Clint left, the bell above the door chimed. Rose was tidying up a stack of cereal boxes, accidentally nudged out of place as Clint left. She looked up to check who had entered.

To her horror, Ash and the big man in the leather jacket stood in front of her. She wasn't expecting them until much later. She waited nervously for them to ask her for the money, unsure what to say. All the while, she frantically racked her brain for some way of wiggling out of her predicament.

"Well?" Ash's friend held out his hand towards her. She wondered how to find out his name.

Rose was sure he didn't want to shake hands. She forced a smile. "I'm very well, thank you, Mr...? Sorry, I don't know your name." The man ignored her. Clearly, he had no intention of giving up that piece of information. She looked him up and down warily. He wore his usual leather jacket. Rose wondered if he ever took it off. The weather was already getting too warm in the middle of the day for a coat. Did he have a knife in one of the pockets? Was that why he always wore it? Her mind flashed back to Roman.

"Where's the money?"

Rose remained silent, wishing the floor would swallow her up.

"I said, where's the sodding money?"

"I don't have it all," Rose said. "It's been a slow morning for business."

The man moved towards her. Rose wanted to run away but saw no point. He would easily catch her before she even got out of the shop. She stood her ground, refusing to show her fear. If he was half decent, he might not want to hit a woman. Rose suspected his decency levels didn't come anywhere near fifty percent.

"Are you taking the mick?"

His raised voice and threatening manner made Rose afraid he would lose control. She reminded herself she was dealing with a couple of animals here, one of whom probably killed Roman. She needed to smooth things over before the situation escalated.

"I'm sorry," she said. "Would you take an instalment, please? It's the best I can do. I couldn't get all of it."

The man grabbed her arm, pulling her towards him until their faces almost touched. "Well, you'd better try a bit harder."

"I'm sorry. I don't have it today." She wanted to tell this man exactly where to get off but decided on a more tactful approach. Images of Roman and her mother filled her head. She didn't want to end up like them, for Jack's sake, and for hers.

"I'll give you one last chance." The man gripped her arm harder. "Tomorrow morning. Don't mess up." He let go of her arm and shoved her in the chest, causing her to topple backwards. The shelves half broke her fall, slowing the speed of descent, but twisting her sideways so she landed heavily on one hip.

"One chance." He kicked her calf, making her flinch with pain.

Rose wanted to cry out, but she bit her tongue and held in the scream. Ash was already heading for the door, not that she'd expected him to help her. She knew exactly where she stood with him. He was equally as bad as his friend.

Rose hardly dared to breathe again until she heard the bell above the shop door and the creak of the hinges as it slowly eased shut.

As soon as they went, Rose's fear turned to anger, mostly anger at herself. How could she let that horrible man push her around like that? Too late, she remembered the self-defence moves Jack taught her at the weekend. Why didn't she remember any of that when it mattered? Not that it would have done any good. With nowhere to run, he would simply have hit her harder. She'd had no choice but to let him win. She must make absolutely sure she got that money for tomorrow. He wouldn't let her off so lightly next time.

She got up slowly, taking stock of her injuries. Hopefully, it would only be bruising, but she might ache for a few days. Her hip screamed in pain where she'd fallen onto the hard floor. It had better not be broken. She didn't have time to get it X-rayed. A trip to Accident and Emergency these days usually involved a five-hour wait, and anyway, the bus ride would be agony. Best to take it easy for the rest of the day, then go home and soak in a hot bath.

Gingerly, she hobbled towards the checkout, opening the barrier before bolting herself in behind the screen. She felt a little safer now. If only she'd been sitting here when those men arrived earlier. But they'd wanted to punish her. They wouldn't have let a screen stop them.

Rose found some packets of aspirin behind the counter and pulled one out. She considered paying for it, but she'd been injured in the course of her job, so it seemed reasonable to take it as a freebie. She swallowed down a couple, chasing them with a few big gulps of water from her bottle, then put the remainder of the aspirin packet into her bag to use later.

Wayne Baker slammed the door of his car shut and started the engine. He almost drove off before Ash finished getting in.

"Hang on a minute, mate." Ash pulled the door shut and reached for his seat belt.

Wayne ignored him, deliberately stamping on the accelerator. That woman had made a fool of him. How dare she refuse to pay him, in front of Ash, too? His reputation would tank if this got out.

"What's with you and the bitch in the shop?" Ash and that woman had acted like they knew each other. Not friends. No, definitely not friends. Too much hostility. But something.

"Nothing," Ash replied. "She's no one."

Wayne didn't believe him. "She recognised you." She didn't exactly say so, but her reaction when Ash walked in said everything. He'd thought as much the last time they came. He should have listened to his gut feeling.

"Maybe she's confusing me with someone else." Ash laughed. "People get me muddled up with my brother all the time. He doesn't even look that much like me."

Wayne pulled out to overtake. He gunned the car up to full speed, flying past the van in front of him. Ash looked white as a ghost. Wayne tapped his fingers casually on the steering wheel before a quick flick of the wrist manoeuvred the car back into the correct lane, moments away from a head-on collision on the wrong side of the road. Except he hadn't been anywhere close to crashing. Not much point in driving a powerful car if you didn't have fun playing with that power, and Ash needed a fright. If anything was going on between Ash and that woman, if Ash was keeping something from him, he'd be getting a much bigger fright than this.

"If the boss finds out you're lying to me, you'll be in big trouble." *Perhaps the same sort of trouble as Terry Thompson.* He'd already got into enough trouble himself for letting this woman negotiate the price down. It had been made very clear to him that the Wolfpack don't negotiate. He knew that. He'd always known that. But the stupid woman made him feel guilty. What was happening to him? He couldn't afford to develop a conscience, not in this job.

Ash looked as if he wanted to tell him something, but the moment passed. "I'm not lying to you," he said. "I wouldn't do that."

"Let's hope not," Wayne said. "We'll go back tomorrow for the rest of the money. She won't give us any trouble, not now."

"No. You scared her proper."

She'd looked terrified. And so she should be. Wayne would never hurt anyone unless they deserved it. But she had disrespected him. That's what made him so angry. No one was allowed to disrespect a member of the Wolfpack and get away with it. She would learn the hard way if she dissed him again.

Chapter 22

By the time Alfie showed up to take over from her, Rose felt much better. A steady stream of customers in the afternoon helped to take her mind off things. It also produced a good bundle of cash. She counted out two hundred pounds.

"We got some visitors this afternoon."

"That's nice." Alfie smiled.

Rose shook her head. "No, it was the men wanting protection money."

"I hope you paid up. I don't want you getting hurt," Alfie said. "At least you negotiated the price down. It might be worse."

Rose flinched. "It is worse. I forgot to tell you they put the price up."

"I thought you negotiated a deal," Alfie said. "I knew that sounded too good to be true."

"They didn't give me any chance to negotiate this time. One of them pushed me onto the floor and kicked me." Even talking about it made her hip ache again, and her calf still felt sore. She was probably due for another couple of aspirins.

Alfie looked concerned. "Are you all right?"

"I'm feeling a bit battered and I'll probably be bruised tomorrow, but nothing major. I've taken some aspirins from the shelf." Rose nodded at the small shelf of medicines they kept behind the counter. "And a hot bath might help."

"I wish I'd been here. I'd have sorted them out for you."

Rose cringed. It was very sweet of Alfie to say that, but he would have got hurt too.

"How much did they want?"

"Two hundred pounds."

"But that's double."

"And it's the same as the original amount they wanted," Rose pointed out.

Alfie looked thoughtful. "I wonder if someone higher up in the gang got angry at them cutting the price for you. If word got out they'd done that, no one would want to pay full price."

"Probably. But we're not in any position to dispute it this time. Look what happened to Roman when he argued with them."

"Did Roman argue with them over the protection money? What makes you say that? Have the police found out something?"

Rose immediately regretted the slip of her tongue. "I just assumed," she said. "Why else would he get stabbed?"

"Round here, plenty of reasons," Alfie said. "But you're probably right. Maybe that's why they backed off so easily and let you negotiate the price down."

"Perhaps they felt guilty about what they'd done," Rose suggested. She mentally kicked herself for being so careless. If those men found out she witnessed the murder, she didn't even want to think about what they might do to her. She also didn't want Alfie and Sarah to find out she'd held back information from the police. How would either of them ever forgive her for that?

"Huh. People like that don't feel guilty."

"Anyway, they're not letting me negotiate anymore. They're coming back tomorrow," Rose said, eager to change the subject. "I've already taken the money out of the till."

"Let me work your shift tomorrow, so I'll be here when they come," Alfie said.

"No," Rose insisted. She needed to face up to this, otherwise she'd be frightened to come to work every day, and she needed the money too much to give up this job. Her credit card bill wouldn't pay itself off. She told herself she could do this, although she still needed to convince herself fully on that score, but she'd be ok by tomorrow. She would have to be.

After a dreadful day, Rose just wanted to get home and eat, followed by a hot bath to ease her aches and pains. She rounded the last corner towards her flat when she saw Darren come out of the building with an older man. Her blood froze as she recognised him: the man who asked her for protection money this morning, the one who roughed her up, the one who she was sure now had been in the shop when Roman was murdered.

The two men were deep in conversation, laughing at something and chatting away like old friends. Darren's friendship with Ash might be a coincidence, but now this other man had been in his flat. Was Darren involved with anything illegal? She should take the chance to warn Tan while Darren was out. If Tan found out what kind of people Darren associated with, maybe she would warn Darren off before he got dragged in too deep.

Walking up the stairs proved painful. Rose quickly got used to the three flights of stairs after she moved in, but now she cursed every step. She'd stiffened up since this morning and ached all over. Her hip still hurt like hell, and she prayed it wasn't broken. She took her time to negotiate the steps, hoping the pain would ease once she took some more aspirins.

Halfway up the stairs, she knocked on Tanya's door.

"Come in. You look terrible. What's up?" Tanya ushered her into her flat.

"I tripped over," Rose lied, immediately realising that now it would be more difficult to explain what she knew about Darren's friend.

"Sit down. I'll make you a cuppa."

"I can't stay," Rose said. "I want to get home. I need a hot bath and a lie down."

"So what's up? If you didn't come in for tea and a chat, what do you want? Are you ok?"

Rose was desperate to get home. She didn't want to drag things out. "Who was that man with Darren?" she asked.

"Oh, that's Wayne. Why are you asking?"

"What's his surname? I thought I recognised him." That wasn't a lie.

"It's Baker, Wayne Baker. I doubt you would know him."

Rose wondered how much to say to her friend. If things were the other way round, if Jack became mixed up with someone like that, she would want Tan to tell her. "He, Wayne, came in the shop earlier. He and Darren's friend Ash have been extorting protection money from us."

Tan laughed. "What, Wayne? He's Darren's cousin. He wouldn't hurt a fly. And Darren's known Ash since school. He would never do anything like that. You must be mistaken."

Rose shook her head. "No. You should be worried that Darren will end up in trouble."

"Yeah, and you should be worried about making up rubbish about my family. I think you should leave." Tanya pointed towards the door. She'd stopped laughing. "Darren can be friends with whoever he likes, as far as I'm concerned. You need to stop poking your nose into our business."

"I'm sorry," Rose said. "I'm trying to help. I thought you'd want to know."

"Nothing to know. You've got it wrong. Now sod off."

Chapter 23

Rose shut the door behind her as soon as she got back to her flat and sank onto the floor in the hallway. She never should have rushed in and told Tanya about Wayne. If only she'd taken more time to find out his connection to her and Darren. She realised how little she really knew about Tan. Hopefully, Tanya would calm down by tomorrow and forgive her. She'd only been trying to help. Surely, Tan would see that?

After a few minutes of wallowing in self-pity, Rose tried to get up. It was a struggle. She propped herself against the wall to get back on her feet. It would take at least a couple more aspirins to dull the pain before she risked getting in the bath, in case she stiffened up and got stuck. In any case, the water needed some time to warm up.

Yet again, Rose suffered a disturbed night's sleep. Lack of sleep was becoming normal these days, but at least this time, she had a legitimate physical reason for her unrest. Her hip still pained her dreadfully, and each time she turned onto her right side, the pain forced her to roll straight back over again.

Halfway through the night, she woke in a sweat from her short doze. She'd been having a nightmare about Jack latching onto Wayne Baker as an elder brother. Jack would be staying with her for most of the summer. She refused to risk her son. His newfound friendship with Darren seemed doomed to land him in trouble. If Darren was involved with the local gangs, she didn't want Jack fraternising with him. But how could she stop Jack? He'd reached that age when he believed he knew best, when he didn't like being told what to do. Like all nineteen-year-olds, he thought he knew it all but, in reality, his naivety worried Rose. Jack still lacked that essential life experience that would ultimately destroy his innocent trust of strangers but would keep him safe.

She wondered which of her nightmares would be worse. Jack getting arrested, or Jack getting murdered. A vivid memory of Roman Marek flew into her head. Getting murdered would be unthinkable. There would be no way back from that. She would do anything to make sure she didn't lose her boy.

When the alarm clock sounded at 6:15 a.m., Rose felt like she'd done battle with a ten-ton truck during the night. Her body ached, and the sharp pain in her hip made her want to throw up every time she moved too quickly. The lack of sleep drew a blanket of fog over her brain and she realised she'd be struggling to function by the end of the day.

Rose made herself a strong cup of tea, wishing she had some coffee instead. There might be more caffeine in a cup of coffee to keep her awake. Swallowing two more aspirins, she washed them down with a burning hot gulp of tea. She left it to cool while she returned to the bedroom to get dressed. Everything took much longer this morning. It would get easier once the aspirin kicked in, but if she waited, she would be late for work.

As she walked to the shop, her problems whirled around in her brain. She had a limited number of choices, all of them bad. Perhaps the most sensible thing to do would be to tell the police what she knew about Wayne. It would help to protect Jack, and she'd do anything for him. But how could she prevent any fallout for herself? An anonymous phone call or letter to tip them off might work, but she doubted the police would take that seriously. At least, she would have all day to consider the problem more carefully. Perhaps by the end of the day, she would come up with a better solution.

Clint showed up early this morning. "Did you hear about the body in Eastbury Park?" he asked excitedly.

"Yes, I went over there yesterday." She'd seen enough dead bodies recently to last her a lifetime. She didn't want to hear about it. She carried on rearranging jars of coffee on the shelves while Clint prattled on.

"Turns out it's Terry Thompson. He went missing a few days ago."

Rose's ears pricked up. "Terry Thompson?"

"Yes, do you know him?" Clint asked.

Rose tried to calm herself. "No," she said, "but I've heard of him." Terry Thompson might be the only real witness to Roman's murder because she refused to count herself, since she didn't actually *see* it happening.

"You'll be hearing a bit more now. Apparently, he got shot in the head."

"Really? How do you know that?" Rose wondered if Clint would come out with any more useful information.

Clint tapped his nose. "I have my sources," he said. "He got shot from behind, too. What sort of coward does that?"

Rose stopped listening. Was this the same Terry who witnessed Roman Marek being stabbed? There wasn't much hope of the police ever finding Roman's killer with Terry, the sole real witness, dead. She was convinced now the murderer must be Darren's cousin, Wayne. She thought she recognised his voice that first time she saw him on the stairs to her flat. Did he kill Terry too? Would he kill her if he found out she knew what he'd done? If she wanted to tell the police, it needed to be soon, before Wayne killed anyone else, before he killed her.

By 6:00 p.m., Rose was as tired and achy as she'd expected, but she forced herself to get on a bus into Brackford. If she didn't go to the police station today, she'd probably change her mind by tomorrow. She ignored her exhaustion. She had to do this, and she couldn't risk the police visiting her at home, or in the shop, in case someone saw them. If Tan or Darren spotted them going into her flat, she might end up like Terry Thompson.

As soon as she got near the police station, Rose started to have an anxiety attack. The sight of the building brought back too many memories of being threatened by Jordan Taylor and struggling to get the police to arrest him for her mother's murder. She still didn't know if she was doing the right thing now. It terrified her that she would be putting herself in the firing line if Wayne Baker found out she grassed on him. It all came back to Jack. Rose could never stand by and risk Jack being harmed, or worse still, being dragged into a life of gangland crime.

She approached the desk. "I need to speak to Detective Inspector Waterford, please." She didn't want to involve DC Farrier. From her dealings with him so far, she worried he wouldn't take her seriously enough and may inadvertently put her in more danger.

The desk sergeant tapped his keyboard and looked at his computer screen. Rose half hoped that DI Waterford wouldn't be in the station today, giving her a good excuse to change her mind and go home.

"I'll see if he's free. What's your name?" the desk sergeant asked.

"Rose Marsden." She wondered if DI Waterford would remember her.

"Take a seat."

Rose sat down, nervously glancing at the other people in the waiting room. If anyone saw her here... The repercussions didn't bear thinking about. She waited, wringing her hands together, wishing she could get up and walk out of this place. But leaving now wouldn't protect Jack.

"Rose Marsden?" A young woman approached her.

"Yes, that's me."

"The inspector will be down shortly. Follow me, please," she said.

Rose followed the woman into a small interview room.

"Can I get you anything to drink?"

Rose remembered the standard of the coffee here. She shook her head. "No, thank you."

Detective Inspector Waterford entered the room. "Mrs Marsden, how are you?"

To Rose's relief, he seemed to remember her, or maybe the desk sergeant briefed him well. "I've got some information," she said. Part of her still wanted to run away.

DI Waterford sat down opposite her. "Fire away."

"I'm not sure where to start." Rose had been going over everything in her head for the last few hours, and still she wasn't certain.

DI Waterford smiled, instantly putting her more at ease. "The beginning is usually the best place."

"Ok." Rose wished she'd asked for that drink now, if only to give her something to do with her hands. "I had to come back from Manchester." She didn't need to give him the details of what Philip had done. "Then Roman got murdered."

"Roman Marek?"

"Yes. Anyway, now I'm working in his shop. I needed a job, and his wife needed help." Rose realised she was just giving the edited highlights, glossing over all the important details. She could fill that in later.

"So what's this got to do with me? Do you have any information about the murder?" DI Waterford asked.

He'd hit the nail on the head. Rose ignored the question and carried on. "Some men are extorting protection money from us."

DI Waterford looked interested. "Go on."

Rose told him about Ash and Wayne, and how Wayne roughed her up and threatened her.

"Do you have any proof, or any independent witnesses?" DI Waterford looked concerned.

Rose shook her head, worried now that this would turn into a repeat of the Jordan Taylor fiasco, where the police knew he'd done it, but initially couldn't touch him for lack of evidence. She should have thought of that before she came here.

"So what about their surnames? I think I know who you mean. They're both known to the police, but we need you to give us more if we're going to do anything about them."

"I don't know Ash's surname," Rose said. Tan could probably tell her, but she could hardly ask her now, not when she wasn't even sure Tan ever wanted to speak to her again. Besides, Tan would go straight back to Wayne Baker and tell him. If only she'd known earlier that Baker was family. "The other one is Wayne Baker."

DI Waterford nodded knowingly. "Could you identify them? Would you recognise them in a police line-up?"

"Yes. Would that be enough to arrest them?" Would it be enough to protect Jack?

"It might be, but it would be easier with more evidence."

Rose steeled herself. She would have to tell him. "Wayne Baker killed Roman Marek," she said.

DI Waterford remained silent. He seemed to be waiting for her to say more.

"I was in the shop when it happened. I was right at the back when they came in, so they never saw me."

"I read the report," Waterford said. "But you said you didn't see anything."

"I was scared, after the stuff with Jordan Taylor."

"That's understandable. So, tell me, what did you see?"

Rose took a deep breath. She had to do this, for Jack's sake. "I heard more than I saw. I mean, I only saw a little in the security mirror. There were two men. One of them, Wayne Baker, stabbed Roman. I've met him since, and I recognised his voice. And I believe the other man was Terry Thompson."

DI Waterford sat up suddenly. "Terry Thompson's been murdered," he said.

Rose nodded. "I heard. Do you think he was killed to keep him quiet? He was a witness." Would she end up the same way?

"It's possible," Waterford said.

"You must promise to keep my name confidential," Rose said.

"We'll try. Is there anywhere else you can stay for a while?"

Rose laughed nervously. What planet did this man live on? It was a miracle she'd got anywhere to live at all. She didn't have the option of staying anywhere else. Besides, there was her job to consider. If she didn't show up to run the shop every day, she'd be letting down Sarah, and she'd be back to having no income again. "No, there's nowhere. And I'll be working in the shop every day." If it got out that she'd given the police this information, she may as well paint a massive target on her back.

DI Waterford looked concerned. "That might be a problem. Can you take some holiday?"

Rose shook her head. "I've only just started, and there's no one to cover for me." Alfie would never manage single-handed. She started to regret coming here. It had been a stupid idea. Whatever made her think she could take on Wayne Baker and win? If he'd shot Terry Thompson, what would he do to her?

"Leave it with me," Waterford said.

"What do I do when Wayne and Ash come back?"

"Just act normally, but be careful. Try not to put yourself in a vulnerable position."

Rose stood up. She'd really hoped the police would be more helpful, that they'd rush straight out and arrest Wayne and Ash. She should have known better.

"I mean it," DI Waterford said. "Be careful." He handed her his card. "Call me anytime, day or night."

Rose dropped the card into her handbag. Fat lot of good that would do her. She needed a better plan.

Chapter 24

Paul Waterford went back upstairs to his office. He now had a suspect, Wayne Baker, for both the Terry Thompson and the Roman Marek murders, but no real evidence for either. Perhaps if Rose Marsden testified, they might get a conviction. But he knew how these things worked around here. Someone would threaten her, if she was lucky. If she was unlucky, they might kill her. She looked as if she would fold easily. It wouldn't take much of a threat to scare her off as a witness. Then Baker would get off scot-free, like he always did.

It worried Paul that Rose worked in the local convenience store. That made her easily accessible. Perhaps they should increase the police presence on the Hale Hill Estate. Except, when they tried that before, it did more harm than good. Some of the residents didn't like uniform presence in the area. It caused a lot of extra tension. Plus, they took every opportunity to slash the patrol car's tyres and treat the uniformed officers like scum. With tension running high on the last occasion they tried it, they were lucky not to start a riot.

He considered putting some plain clothes officers on the ground in the estate. Unfortunately, most of the career criminals knew everyone in CID. There might be a couple of officers in the murder investigation team who didn't visit the estate enough to be recognised. But with two murders to investigate, he would struggle to spare anyone. He guessed he would have to, otherwise there might be a third murder soon, and he didn't want that on his conscience.

"What we need is some real evidence." Rose spent all day mulling over the problem in her mind. It might be the only way to stop Wayne and Ash, get the police involved and get them arrested on charges that would stick.

Alfie sighed. "You can't take on this gang. It's too dangerous. Why can't you see that, after everything they've done in the last few weeks?"

Rose banged her fist on the wall, exasperated. "I have to do something." No way could she sit around and do nothing, with the very real danger that Jack would either get targeted and badly hurt or killed, or he would get sucked into the gangs and end up in prison, if he didn't get killed first. She wouldn't take that risk. Somehow, she needed to protect him, and the only way to do that was to find some very real evidence against Ash and Wayne Baker.

"But these people don't play by the rules. Do you want to get killed?"

"Of course I don't, but I don't want Jack killed either." Rose would do anything to protect her son. Why didn't Alfie understand that?

"So, what if you do manage to take down a couple of them? Two more will just spring up in their place. You realise that, don't you?"

"Then I'll take down the next two, and the next." She and Alfie might never agree on this, but she needed his help.

"They think they're above the law, that's the trouble, and they probably are. The police are scared to come onto the estate."

That attitude, and the resulting apathy among the local residents, had empowered the gang in the first place and now that same reluctance to stand up to them made the gang stronger. "Well, are you going to help me or not? Surely you don't want to see Roman's murderer get away with it?"

"Of course not." Alfie looked embarrassed.

"Then how are we going to get some evidence?"

Alfie sat down with an enormous sigh. "I'll help you because it's the only way to shut you up, but I'm warning you, you need to be really careful."

The bell above the door tinkled, and the conversation paused instantly.

"Clint. What can I do for you today?" Alfie asked.

"Just a pint of milk," Clint said, shuffling towards the other end of the shop.

Rose paced up and down near the door, frustrated at the interruption. She had no idea if Alfie would find a solution to her problem, but he sounded as if he might come up with a plan of some sort, so she was impatient to hear it. He'd better not change his mind about helping her.

Clint usually wanted to stay and chat for ages, but to Rose's relief, he left quickly for once.

"Evidence," Rose reminded Alfie. "You were just about to come up with a brilliant scheme to get evidence of the protection racket."

"Was I?" Alfie smiled at her. "I hoped you might have forgotten."

"No chance." Rose smiled back, then locked her eyes onto his. She wouldn't let him off the hook.

"Ok," Alfie said. "So, for a start, we can use what we've got. Those new CCTV cameras will record everything. You just need to make sure these men are facing the camera at some point."

"How do I do that?"

"You'll have to work that one out for yourself," Alfie said. "But if you're sitting at the checkout, chances are the camera will get a good view of their faces."

"What if they get suspicious of the cameras?" Rose asked. She worried they might try to smash their new CCTV system.

"It won't happen," Alfie said. "They've already seen the cameras loads of times, and they think they're broken. As long as you don't keep looking at either of the cameras, it won't occur to them that we might have replaced them. The new cameras are identical to the old ones."

"Will it be enough to get them on camera?" After what DI Waterford said, Rose was paranoid that she wouldn't manage to capture enough evidence to get Ash and Wayne convicted.

"No, probably not. But we're going to record them, as well."

"They'll see me if I try to do it on my phone," Rose pointed out.

Alfie laughed. "This new-fangled technology is useless. I've got a good old-fashioned tape recorder at home."

Rose made a face at him. "It must be an antique," she said.

"Don't be so cheeky. It's a good bit of kit, and it records for a lot longer than your phone will."

"Sorry." She didn't want to put Alfie off by being disrespectful when he was trying to help her.

"I'll bring it in tomorrow and set it up. All you'll have to do is hit the button as soon as you see them coming. If you leave it too late, they might hear the click as it turns on."

Rose was buoyed up now that they had a feasible plan. It sounded as if it would work. The combination of getting the men's faces on video and recording everything they said ought to be enough. She would have to steer the conversation in the right direction, so that they mentioned on tape about asking for the money. If they threatened her on tape, so much the better. Rose's spirits were lifted by actually doing something positive. She just wished it wasn't taking so long. She would be on tenterhooks until tomorrow.

Chapter 25

Alfie showed up just after 7:00 a.m. with his old-fashioned tape recorder. "Don't laugh," he said. "It'll do the job." He pressed the record button. Nothing happened.

"Doesn't it work? Perhaps I should use my phone after all," Rose said.

"No." Alfie made a face at her. "I'll fix it." He unscrewed the back of the machine. "Damn. There's a loose wire."

"Let me see." Rose turned the tape recorder towards her to get a better look before handing it back to him. "Mind the shop for me. I'll be ten minutes." She ran out before Alfie got the chance to ask where she was going.

Rose returned in less than ten minutes. She opened her bag and took out the items she had fetched from home.

"That's a dinky little soldering iron," Alfie said. "I've never seen one that size."

"I use it for making jewellery," Rose explained. "It should be pretty easy to fix that loose wire."

It didn't take long for Rose to mend the tape recorder. She gave it a few minutes for the solder to set properly, then pushed the record button. The machine whirred into action.

"Well done, that's a very professional job." Alfie wound the cassette back to the beginning before duct taping the machine underneath the counter, conveniently placed for Rose to switch it on easily when the men came in. They would never spot it there.

"All set." Alfie tapped the counter, making Rose fearful that the duct tape wouldn't hold and the machine would crash to the floor. "It's all up to you now," he said.

Rose ducked down to check his handiwork. She needn't have worried. The tape recorder remained firmly taped in position.

"Right, I'm going back to bed." Alfie headed towards the door. "It's way too early for me. However do you get up so early every day?"

Rose was a bundle of nerves for the rest of the morning, waiting for Wayne and Ash to show up. When they finally arrived, it almost came as a relief. Quickly, she bent down and flicked the switch on the tape recorder, ordering herself to stay calm.

"You got the money?" Wayne Baker poked his hand through the opening in the bottom of the Perspex screen.

Rose resisted the temptation to slap it. It wouldn't do her any good and would only make the situation much worse. "Yes. Remind me how much you're demanding."

"Two hundred."

"You can't keep coming in and bleeding us dry like this. What gives you the right to take our money? It's stealing." Rose took a breath, determined to see this through, to make at least one of them admit enough to prove that they operated an illegal protection racket. She needed this evidence sewn up as tightly as possible.

Wayne leaned forwards and pressed his face against the screen, squashing his features so he looked like he should be in a fairground attraction. If it weren't for the screen, his face would almost be touching hers. Rose recoiled from him.

"I'll do what I sodding well like." Wayne stood up straight and stepped back. "Now give me the money before I let Ash loose on you, or do you want to end up like the Polish guy?"

Ash busied himself fiddling with some cans of soup on the shelves. Hearing his name, he picked one up, tossing it in the air and catching it again. Rose's nerves were already shredded, especially after hearing Wayne admit that one of them was responsible for Roman Marek's murder. Ash scared her as much as Wayne did. If he threw one of those cans at her, he'd do some serious damage. Rose glanced towards where the tape recorder silently whirred away out of sight beneath the counter. She really needed to get Ash's voice on it too, admitting to something. But attracting him over here was a bad idea when he held a heavy can of soup that he might use as a weapon.

"Do you want to pay for that soup?" she called across the shop.

Ash turned around and tossed the can of soup at her. Rose ducked as it hit the edge of the screen, glancing off and falling on the floor.

Rose bit her lip to stop herself from smiling. He'd done that in full view of the CCTV camera. She opened the till and took out the envelope of cash she had placed there earlier, opening it and counting out the notes in front of them. With any luck, perhaps this would be the last time, if these men didn't simply get replaced by two worse ones. She glanced towards the tape recorder again.

"What you got in there?" Ash walked towards her. He reached over and unbolted the gate, pushing his way into the small space next to her behind the till.

"You're not allowed in here," Rose said, trying to sound confident.

"You're not allowed in here." Ash parodied her. "I'm not your little mummy's boy. I'll do what I like."

"Lay off, Ash. Let's take the money and go."

For a moment, Rose was grateful to Wayne Baker for intervening.

"She's hiding something under there." Ash bent down and reached under the counter. He gave a tug, pulling the tape recorder from its hiding place. He lost his grip on it, and it fell to the floor, pieces of duct tape drifting from its edges. "Bloody hell. What sort of ancient rubbish is this? Ain't you ever heard of an iPhone?" He pressed all the buttons, one by one. The tape recorder ceased recording, then it popped open, ejecting its contents.

"Have you been recording us?" Wayne asked angrily.

"Reckon she needs teaching a lesson," Ash said. He removed the cassette and pulled the tape out, screwing it up into a spaghetti of brown plastic. He stuffed it in his pocket.

Rose's heart thumped frantically against her rib cage. Ash pinned her in, leaving no way to escape from behind the counter. Even if she did, Wayne would be waiting for her. Already, she seriously regretted this stupid plan. Whatever made her believe she could win this battle? Why didn't she just leave it all to the police? But she knew exactly why. She would risk everything if it meant protecting her son from harm.

"Just take the money and go." Thinking of Jack strengthened Rose's resolve. She thrust the bundle of notes towards Ash. It pained her to hand over the cash, but it wasn't worth getting hurt for any amount of money. A sharp twinge in her calf overshadowed the constant pain in her hip to remind her what would happen if she didn't cooperate. Perhaps it would happen anyway, given Ash had found the tape recorder. She pressed her hands onto the counter to stop them from shaking.

Ash snatched the money from her, stuffing it into his pocket. He reached across Rose to the open till, pushing her roughly against the counter, and emptied the contents of the till into his pockets.

Rose's fear of taking a beating hit a new height. She'd never been more grateful to hear the tinkling of the bell over the door. Ash picked up the tape recorder, ramming it into Rose's chest before tossing it onto the floor.

"Ash. Come on," Wayne commanded, already moving towards the door as two women entered the shop.

Ash followed him, ducking past the women, and started running.

Chapter 26

Alfie came as soon as Rose phoned him.

"They found the tape recorder," Rose said the moment Alfie walked through the door.

"Damn." Alfie thumped his fists against the wall.

"We might still find something useful on the CCTV," Alfie said. "Give me your phone. I'll download the footage."

Alfie's presence calmed Rose. Those men were less likely to come back with two of them here. "Can you see them on the video?" Rose shouted in the direction of the storeroom, where Alfie watched the CCTV footage. She needed to stay in the shop to keep an eye out in case any customers came in.

"You can watch it in a minute," Alfie called back.

A few minutes later, he returned with her phone. He held it up so they could both view it and tapped the play button on the video.

"See this bit here." Alfie pointed at the small screen in front of them. "Can you remember what Baker said then?"

"He told me to give him the money." Rose didn't see what good that would do, with no sound on the CCTV camera.

"If the police can get a lip-reader to watch it, they might be able to make out the words." He fast forwarded the video. "You can see Ash throwing a can at you. It's not much, but it's worth giving the video to the police. If it gets them off our backs, it will be worth doing."

Rose didn't want to ruin his mood by reminding him of what she kept telling her, that the gang would soon find two replacements and they'd be right back to the beginning. But at least this might give them a few weeks' respite.

"I'll take it to them as soon as I finish work." Rose replaced her phone in her pocket. "I don't want the police coming here. It's too obvious. Wayne and Ash will find out I told them."

"I agree," Alfie said.

"Or you could take it to the police station now," Rose suggested.

"No. It has to be you," Alfie insisted.

"Why?"

"You were here when they came. I wasn't. I'll cover the shop for you so you can go right away. The sooner we do this, the better."

"Thank you." Alfie was right. She needed to do this now. If she left it any longer, she might lose her nerve.

Rose took the bus straight to the police station. Luckily, Detective Inspector Waterford agreed to see her immediately.

"You told me you needed evidence," Rose said.

DI Waterford suddenly looked interested. "I take it this is about the protection racket."

"Yes, and possibly also Roman Marek's murder." Rose had the CCTV footage with her. She hoped it would be enough.

DI Waterford perked up even further. "What do you have for me?"

Rose handed over the memory stick with the CCTV recording on it. "I recorded it too, but Ash destroyed the recording. I can tell you what they said, and if you have a lip reader, they may be able to get some of it from the CCTV. Wayne Baker practically confessed to Roman Marek's murder."

Rose ran through her conversation with Wayne Baker. "Is it enough? Will you be able to arrest both men and charge them now?" Rose held her breath. She had been here before, on the verge of getting a dangerous criminal locked up, only to see it all fall through because of weak evidence. She didn't want a repeat performance of that. Silently, she cursed herself for giving away the location of the tape-recorder to Ash.

"We'll need to review this thoroughly. I don't want to get your hopes up."

Rose shook her head in despair.

"I understand what you've been through before, being unable to get proper justice for your mother's murder," DI Waterford said. "That's why I won't make any promises, but I'll do my best."

"Thank you." Rose wondered if it would come to anything. It wasn't right that these people kept getting away with their crimes. They shouldn't be allowed to intimidate people and extort money from hardworking small business owners. They shouldn't be allowed to get away with murder either.

Chapter 27

DI Paul Waterford checked his watch: 5:05 a.m. He fastened his bulletproof vest. They weren't taking any chances. A full team of armed response officers waited outside Wayne Baker's house, ready to arrest him. Another team would simultaneously pick up Ashley Walker from where he lived on the other side of Brackford. Rose Marsden came up trumps with her CCTV footage. When they found a lip-reader to watch the video footage she'd given him, Wayne Baker had dropped himself in it up to his neck and incriminated Ashley Walker as well. It gave them enough reason to justify a pre-dawn raid on both of their houses.

"Stand by," he said quietly into the microphone on his wrist. The whole team wore earpieces and were waiting for Paul to give the go ahead. "Enter on my command. Make it fast and make it safe. Don't forget Baker may be armed." He dialled a number on his phone.

Detective Sergeant Barry Medway picked up. "Guv?"

Paul spoke into his phone and his wrist mike at once. "Go, go, go."

The armed response team sprang into action, moving towards Baker's front door with the stealth of a herd of gazelles. At the back of Baker's garden, more members of the team would be ready in case he tried to escape over the fence. Barry's team would be mirroring the manoeuvres in North Brackford at Ashley Walker's house.

A loud bang disturbed the silence as one of the team rammed the enforcer into the front door. In his earpiece, multiple officers shouting, "armed police," nearly deafened Paul. Then heavy footsteps muffled the voices as the herd of gazelles morphed into rhinos.

A dog barked ferociously from somewhere inside the house. Paul began to worry. He didn't realise Wayne Baker owned a dog. Someone must have slipped up, failed to carry out surveillance properly. Maybe the dog wasn't as big or fierce as it sounded. Paul hoped no one would shoot the dog. That would be a PR nightmare.

He listened intently, trying to pick out any sound that told him they'd captured Baker. It always frustrated him being on the outside like this. He would miss all the action. Unarmed himself, Paul wouldn't enter the house until he got the all clear from the armed response team, until Wayne Baker was safely in handcuffs.

"He's gone out the back," the shout came through Paul's earpiece. Paul shifted position to get a better view, while remaining under cover of the car. It hadn't been possible to get into the garden earlier, but the team at the back would get Baker if he climbed over the garden fence.

A barrage of swear words assaulted Paul's ears. "He's in the neighbour's garden. We can't get over the fence."

"Left or right neighbour?" Paul asked.

"Left."

Paul moved position again to get a better view of the property on the left of Baker's house. "Get out of the house. He's at number sixty-six." Paul waited, holding his breath. Three armed men rushed out the door at number sixty-four and pointed their weapons towards number sixty-six. Paul shuddered. They were trained to be careful, not to put innocent civilians in harm's way unnecessarily, but the risks had just skyrocketed. Anyone might be in that house, elderly people, or children. He prayed for this to end well.

Frustrated, Paul waited for Wayne Baker to leave number sixty-six. What if he climbed another fence and got into number sixty-eight's garden? Or he might have got into the house and be holding its occupants as hostages. Once again, Paul longed to be in the thick of the action, but as a detective inspector, his job was to take command. Someone needed to retain an overview of the situation and give orders.

In his peripheral vision, he caught a sign of movement and flicked his head around quickly to check. A man came out from the side of number sixty-two, walking rapidly away from them. Paul took a second look. Wearing black made it difficult in the darkness to be sure if it was him, but the bulky outline of the man's figure suggested it might be Wayne Baker. The man broke into a run. Paul sprinted in his direction.

"Suspect fleeing on foot towards Connell Lane," he spoke into his wrist mike. "Urgent assistance required." Paul picked up speed as Baker realised he was being pursued. Paul hadn't asked if Baker was armed. Too late now. He would have to rely on his bulletproof vest to protect him. If he kept up this pace, Baker wouldn't have time to stop and focus enough to get a head shot. Hopefully, someone would be pursuing in a vehicle by now. They would need to be because Baker seemed to be running like an Olympic athlete.

Paul pumped his arms and ran faster. Baker had nearly reached the corner already. Paul couldn't risk losing sight of him for long. He'd heard nothing in his earpiece, so he didn't know if backup was coming or not. His breathing was too laboured for him to speak now, so he would have to trust that help was on its way.

He thought he'd been gaining on Baker, but fear seemed to give the man's feet wings. Paul needed to make up ground faster or he'd lose him for sure. In front of him, Baker rounded the corner, disappearing from sight for several seconds. If only Paul could second-guess Baker's intentions, he might find a shortcut to head him off.

He put in a spurt of effort and turned the corner, just in time to see Baker duck into an alleyway further ahead. Brackford was littered with alleyways, a confusing network of shortcuts throughout the town. Several years ago, Paul operated in this part of Brackford, and when he'd been a police constable, he'd spent a few weeks running daily in this area, partly as fitness training, partly to familiarise himself with all the shortcuts. Delving into his memory, he felt sure the next footpath along fed in diagonally to the alleyway Baker just took. If Paul ran fast enough, he may be able to cut Baker off and surprise him. Ignoring the searing heat in his lungs, Paul pushed himself harder. He lengthened his stride and flew up the footpath, hoping that nothing would trip him up in the semi-darkness.

Chapter 28

DS Barry Medway watched with excitement as armed police broke down Ashley Walker's front door. He'd given the order to go as soon as he got the call from the DI. As he watched the last officer disappear through the doorway, he anticipated a quick result. He couldn't wait to get in there and join in the action.

He counted up to ten, trying to be patient. The armed response unit got all the excitement. If the opportunity came up, he might apply to join their team.

"Eight, nine, ten," he whispered under his breath.

"We got him, guv."

Barry's adrenaline dissipated instantly. The arrest was almost too easy, although, of course, the guv would be pleased that they'd apprehended Walker. He waited for the armed unit officers to bring Walker out of the house. There was a nice cell back at the station with his name on it. Best to get him in there fast.

Trying to summon up some patience, Barry waited a few minutes before he phoned Paul Waterford. If Paul's phone rang at a vital moment, Barry would get a bollocking, and rightly so if it screwed up the operation. He definitely wouldn't rush. No way would they have captured Baker with the slick efficiency Barry had overseen here. They would compare notes once both prisoners were safely ensconced in the holding cells. The comparison would make Barry look good. He smiled at the prospect.

It was much darker on the footpath away from any street lighting, but Paul's eyes were finally growing accustomed to the lack of light. He neared the branch in the path, where it tapered into the alleyway Baker was using. As soon as Paul reached the fork, he stopped and looked in both directions. A shadowy figure fled down the path away from him. Damn. Baker had turned around and doubled back. He must have heard Paul's footsteps coming along the track towards him.

Paul forced himself to carry on, racing after Baker. He lifted his wrist up to his mouth. "Heading towards Connell Lane from the footpath, five hundred metres from the junction." His words came out in a staccato between each laboured breath. "Where's my backup?"

All Paul Waterford heard was the rhythm of his footsteps thudding against the tarmac and the wheezy sound of his own breath. He put a hand to his ear. "Bollocks," he cursed, catching a breath. His earpiece was missing. It must have worked loose while running. Perhaps he hadn't been careful enough putting it in earlier. How long ago did he last have his earpiece? He couldn't remember. Did his team receive any of his requests for help, or any of the updates about his location?

Baker had almost reached the road, the street light illuminating him enough for Paul to verify his identity. A sprinkling of traffic on the road beyond produced more light, as each pair of headlights dazzled the spot in front of Baker before fading rapidly into nothing. He hoped Baker wouldn't run out in front of a car and get hit.

Paul put in a huge spurt of effort. He was much fitter than the clearly tiring Wayne Baker and gained ground rapidly now.

As soon as Baker reached the road, he stopped and doubled over, struggling for breath. Paul would soon catch him. Only a few more strides. More headlights lit up Wayne Baker as he stood upright. Suddenly, instead of passing by, the car slammed its brakes on, skidding to a stop with an ear-piercing screech.

For a moment, Paul thought Baker might have been hit, but he kept moving towards the vehicle. Paul was so close now. He launched himself at Baker, leaping through the air so his momentum would take down the much larger man. In that split second, the car began to move, and Wayne Baker was pulled onto the back seat through the open door. As the car sped off, Paul landed heavily on the tarmac.

What just happened? He answered his own question as he picked himself up and stared after the taillights of the disappearing car. Already, it was too far away for him to make out the registration number. Paul shrugged. They were probably false plates, anyway. He pulled out his phone and speed dialled the sergeant in charge of the armed response team.

The sergeant answered his phone immediately. "Where are you? Baker's disappeared."

"I've been chasing him. I lost him on Connell Lane. He got into a car, a silver BMW." Paul decided not to waste time explaining the loss of his earpiece. That fiasco would come out when he reported back to the DCI later this morning. It would probably be overlooked, against the bigger fiasco of someone not knowing his right from his left, concentrating everyone's focus onto number 66, while Baker legged it away from number 62.

"Can somebody pick me up, please?" Paul asked.

"Right, sir. I'll be with you in five minutes."

Paul brushed the grit from his jeans. At least they would get a chance to discuss what went wrong during the drive back to the station.

Back at the station, DI Paul Waterford's frustration grew. He was still embarrassed about letting Wayne Baker escape, even though it wasn't entirely his fault. That stupid young DC didn't muddle up his left and right, but he'd been facing in a completely different direction to Paul when he'd given the instruction to go left instead of right. At least Barry's team had arrested Ashley Walker.

Barry met him outside the interview room.

"Has he said anything yet?" Paul asked.

"Not really," Barry said. "Just keeps saying we've got the wrong man."

"They all say that." It was a standard excuse. Most of the local criminals used it at one time or another. "Is his solicitor here yet?"

Barry nodded, resting his hand on the door handle. "Duty solicitor's taking it."

That wasn't a good sign. In Paul's experience, members of the Wolf-pack gang generally used an expensive private solicitor. If no one was willing to pay for his services to defend Ashley Walker, in all likelihood, Walker didn't know anything of any use. Again, he regretted letting Wayne Baker slip away from him.

Barry opened the door. They sat down opposite Walker and the duty solicitor and introduced themselves.

"This is clearly a case of mistaken identity." The duty solicitor leaned back in his chair. "This gentleman is not Ashley Walker. This is his younger brother, Mitch."

Paul had never met Ashley Walker. He looked at Barry.

"Prove it," Barry said, addressing Ashley. "Because you look remarkably like him to me. Do you have any ID on you?"

Ashley would have been searched at the time of arrest, so Paul didn't expect him to produce any ID.

"We're requesting that this interview is suspended until we are able to procure suitable identification documents." The solicitor reached for his briefcase, clearly assuming the interview to be over.

Paul didn't have any choice but to grant his request. In any case, he had better things to do than waste his time interviewing the wrong suspect because his gut feeling told him that Mitch Walker was telling the truth. "Take him back to custody, DS Medway. Make sure I'm informed if they produce proof of ID." He got up and left the room, in no mood to sort out this mess. Let Barry deal with his own screw-up.

He returned to his office and started a search on his computer. Ashley Walker did indeed have a younger brother called Mitch. A quick study of the photos revealed that the two brothers looked very much alike. At five o'clock in the morning, it may have been a reasonable mistake to make. At least it put his own balls up with Baker into perspective, but it didn't change the fact that neither of the men was in custody, and the team was nowhere near solving the murders of either Roman Marek or Terry Thompson. As soon as Barry came back to the office, he'd get him on to sounding out his informants. Perhaps one of them would tell Barry where to find Baker or Walker.

Chapter 29

Rose was in the middle of eating a sandwich when Jack phoned at lunchtime.

"Hi, Mum. I'm leaving home soon. I should be with you in a couple of hours."

"That's great, darling. I'll see you later. Phone me when you get to Brackford station." She'd been looking forward all week to Jack staying this weekend, then at the last minute, he'd phoned to tell her he needed to play in a football match on Saturday morning, substituting for an injured player, and would arrive after lunch. Rose was disappointed at having less time to spend with Jack, but at least he hadn't cancelled the visit. She'd arranged a proper outing for this evening, surprise tickets for the theatre in the West End.

"Ok, will do." Jack hung up.

Rose checked the clock on the wall. Another two hours to wait. She guessed she would be clock watching for the rest of the afternoon. Hopefully, Alfie would remember his offer to start early today. He should be here at 3:00 p.m.

The shop was packed with customers today, making the afternoon pass quickly. When Rose next checked the time, the clock showed two fifty-five already. Good, Alfie should be here any minute now. She started to tidy up, ready to leave the moment Alfie walked through the door. Jack hadn't phoned yet, so the train might have been delayed, or more likely, he'd popped to the shops as soon as he arrived in Brackford.

The bell above the shop door tinkled. Good, that would be Alfie, right on time. Rose let herself out from behind the checkout area, eager to get home before Jack showed up.

As Rose walked across the shop, instead of Alfie, Wayne Baker strode through the doorway, marching towards her as if he owned the place.

Rose stood her ground, confident that he didn't know what she'd done. "Can I help you, sir?" she said, forcing a smile.

Baker glowered at her. "Word is, you've been talking to the police."

"Of course I have." As long as she showed no weakness, she might be ok. "They're still investigating my mother's break-in last month." Inside, Rose's heart pounded at a million miles an hour. She reminded herself to keep breathing.

"Not what I heard." Baker stepped towards her and grabbed her arm, gripping it roughly.

Rose tried to pull away, but Baker's strength overwhelmed her feeble attempt to break free. "Well, it's the truth." She guessed Tanya must have spoken to him, but Tan wouldn't realise she'd been to the police station since their conversation about Darren. Baker must just be guessing, putting two and two together and making at least five or six. She tried to stay calm. Clearly, Baker wasn't stupid, but he couldn't prove anything.

Baker tightened his grip on her arm. "Maybe we'll see what young Jack has to say about it."

"Leave him out of this." Rose didn't care what Baker did to her, as long as he didn't go anywhere near her son.

"I just want a little chat with him, man to man." Baker smiled.

Rose felt sick. "Let go of me," she shouted at him. She needed to get away from Wayne Baker and find Jack before Baker did.

"If you grassed on me, your boy's dead," Wayne hissed. He pulled Rose closer to him, pressing himself against her, holding her in a vice-like grip, too close for her to knee him in the groin.

"I haven't done anything," Rose protested, hoping she sounded sincere. If only she could take half a step back and twist around to get a good angle, she'd be able to put Wayne Baker in his place for long enough to break free and run.

The shop doorbell tinkled. "What's going on here?" Alfie stood behind Baker, looking ready to explode.

Baker turned towards him, still holding Rose's left arm, twisting it behind her until she almost screamed with pain. "Get lost. We're having a private conversation here. It's none of your business."

Rose searched around for anything within reach that she might use to hit Baker. She worried that Alfie would start a fight with him, then she and Alfie would both get hurt.

Alfie stepped towards them. "It is very much my business." He glared angrily at Wayne Baker. "Let go of the lady, or—"

"Or what?" Baker interrupted. "You going to stop me, old man?"

"Can we please talk about this sensibly?" Rose intervened, trying to calm down some of the testosterone in the room. "This is all a misunderstanding."

Baker twisted her arm uncomfortably. "Who asked you?"

Rose yelped. "Let go of me." She glanced pleadingly at Alfie, willing him to fetch help, or phone the police.

Alfie stepped towards them. "You heard the lady."

"Sod off," Baker said. He grasped Rose's arm harder, pinching it painfully.

Rose was torn between wanting Alfie to back off and wanting to escape Baker's grip. Why didn't Alfie just phone the police?

Before Rose got the chance to say anything, Alfie rushed at Baker and thumped him hard in the stomach. Baker immediately let go of Rose and landed a punch slap bang in the centre of Alfie's jaw.

Alfie started raining punches into Baker's face. "Rose, run," he shouted.

For a second, Rose froze to the spot, terrified that Alfie would get hurt on her account.

"RUN," Alfie shouted again. He threw up his right arm, blocking a punch from Baker, then brought his left fist round in an arc and bashed it against Baker's ear. "Get help."

Rose came to her senses. She needed to phone the police. That would be the best way for her to help Alfie, calling the police before

Baker hurt him badly. She ran for the door. As she opened it, she caught sight of Alfie being thrown against the shelving in the middle aisle of the shop. She paused, reluctant to run out on Alfie when he needed her.

Some of the shelving had collapsed and Alfie lay in a heap on the floor, surrounded by cans of tomatoes. Wayne Baker kicked Alfie hard in the leg, then ran towards Rose. Alfie picked up a soup can and launched it at Baker. Rose didn't wait to see if Alfie's missile hit its target. She ran out the door, hurtling down the street as fast as her legs would carry her.

It didn't take long for Rose to realise that Baker had followed her. She ran faster. No way could she risk Baker catching her again. She dreaded to think what might happen if he did.

The street appeared deserted. Rose kept running. Behind her, the thud of Baker's footsteps on the tarmac surface drove her on. She didn't dare look behind her. She tried to decide where to go. It wouldn't be safe to return to her flat. There must be somewhere nearby with lots of people around, but where? The school bus wasn't due yet, and anyone in this area lucky enough to actually have a job would still be at work. There was no sign of anyone who might help her.

Rose ducked into an alleyway, immediately regretting the decision. She was even less likely to find anyone here. Baker would certainly follow her, and if he caught her before she reached the end, he could do anything he wanted to her with no witnesses. Perhaps it was a bad decision on her part, but it would take her to a busier road. She needed to find the safety of other people because she wouldn't manage to outrun Baker for much longer. She hoped Alfie wasn't too injured by Baker to call the police.

The tarmac surface along this alleyway looked badly worn and pitted with holes and stones. She concentrated on avoiding the worst of the potholes, terrified of tripping and falling. Baker seemed to be gaining ground on her. The laboured sound of his breathing became louder. She mustn't let him catch her. Her stomach ached with a stitch. Seeing the end of the alleyway up ahead, she clutched at her stomach and mustered an extra spurt of effort.

Baker shouted something at her but, totally focused on getting away, she failed to make out any words. It sounded like a threat. She didn't want to hear it.

The swish of traffic on the road up ahead beckoned her to pick up speed. Once she made it to the main road, someone might stop to help her. She forced herself to battle on, finding the strength from somewhere inside her. Without warning, her foot hit a lump on the path and she stumbled, flailing her arms to keep her balance. To her relief, she somehow managed to stay upright, but she'd lost ground. Suddenly, a vice-like grip encompassed her right arm, pulling back at her and spinning her around. Wayne Baker held on to her while puffing like crazy to get his breath back.

Terrified, Rose tried to pull away, but Baker held her arm too tightly. She had to do something while he was still at a disadvantage from being breathless. Clearly, he was far less fit than Rose, who recovered her breath quickly, but if she waited any longer, he would recover too. This might be her one chance to protect herself and make sure that Jack would be safe. Jack would be arriving at her flat very soon and she dreaded to think what Wayne Baker might do to him if he found him there.

In a flash of inspiration, Rose remembered what Jack taught her the last time he visited. With her left arm, she slammed her fist into Baker's throat, then whirled around, twisting her right arm to free herself.

Baker sank to his knees, clutching at his throat. Already out of breath from running, now he gasped desperately for air. Rose didn't wait to see if he would be all right. She ran as fast as she could. If she didn't get away now, Baker would never give her the chance to repeat that performance.

Chapter 30

As soon as Rose reached the road, she glanced around quickly, looking for help. The cars she heard earlier had disappeared, leaving the road empty. This wasn't the main road she hoped for, just a minor side-road. She set off at a run again, desperate to get out of sight before Baker recovered enough to follow. She tried to remember how long it took Jack to return to normal after being flicked in the throat. Maybe a couple of minutes, although she hit Baker much harder than she had hit her son. Even so, it would be dangerous to assume Baker's recovery rate would be slower.

She finally got her bearings, recognising the location. Further along the road, a shortcut would take her to the cemetery. That would get her out of sight if Baker came after her. Baker did her a favour by stopping her, enabling her to get her breath back. Now, she flew along, finding hidden reserves of energy.

As she ducked into the footpath, she glanced back to make sure Baker wasn't in pursuit. Thankfully, she saw no sign of him, but she couldn't afford to take off the pressure yet. She kept running, wanting to get as far away from him as possible.

It started to rain. The cool, damp mist on her face provided a welcome relief. But the rain quickly became heavier and Rose wished she'd picked up her coat before she'd left the shop. She would get soaked if it carried on like this for long.

Still worried that Baker might be following, she took a circuitous route to the cemetery. Her stamina began to wane now. She would struggle to keep going much longer without taking a rest.

At last, she reached the main cemetery gates. Once inside, she sheltered under a large tree, its low, leafy branches hiding her well enough, as long as Baker didn't search too thoroughly. The rain lashed down, dripping off the branches in front of her. Perhaps the bad weather would make Baker go home.

Gradually, her breathing returned to normal. The rain still pelted down, flattening the tulips that grew around the edges of the graveyard. Rose leaned against the tree trunk and took out her phone. Quickly, she dialled Jack, trying to think of where he might be safest. She didn't want him going to the flat, in case Baker decided to wait for her to go home.

"Hi, darling." Rose tried to keep her voice calm and normal.

"I'll be home soon," Jack said.

"No," Rose said, failing to keep the anxiety from her voice now. "Don't go to the flat. Wait at the station. I'll come and get you." She had no idea how she would get there as she'd left her purse at the shop, and it was too far to walk. Perhaps she would ask Sarah to pick him up and take him back to her place.

Jack laughed. "Don't worry, Mum. I got Ash to pick me up from the station. I'll be home in a few minutes."

The phone went dead. Rose tried to phone Jack straight back, but it wasn't a lost signal. The low battery sign appeared on the screen. One percent battery. She quickly typed a text to Jack. A few moments later, it pinged back as unsent before the screen went blank.

Rose felt numb. Jack wouldn't be safe with Ashley Walker. Her son would have no idea how much danger he might be in. If only the phone battery hadn't given out at that moment so she could have warned him.

The rain stopped as suddenly as it started. Across the graveyard, Mum's grave stood out, its temporary wooden cross incongruous at the end of a row of smart marble headstones. She walked over to it and knelt on the wet grass.

"I wish you were still here, Mum. You'd tell me what to do." Mum had always been the practical one in an emergency.

The flowers that Rose and Jack bought on their last visit were dead, and the jam jar holding them had toppled over. Rose pulled out the soggy brown remnants of the flowers, ashamed of how long it was since she'd visited Mum's grave. She put them aside. Perhaps she would find a bin or a compost heap somewhere in the graveyard to dump the dead flowers. She carefully stood the jam jar in front of the wooden cross. It would do for next time, and one day she'd replace it with something smarter, a proper vase, the sort of vase her mother deserved.

She was about to get to her feet when a massive punch to her back sent her flying forwards. Instinctively, she put out her hands to save herself. Her left hand whacked painfully into the wooden cross, sending it sideways.

"Bitch." Wayne Baker towered above her. "No one does that to me and gets away with it." He spat on her, making her recoil sharply.

His voice croaked abnormally. Rose didn't know if it was from the unaccustomed exertion or from her punch to his throat.

She shrunk back into the wet ground beneath her, almost wishing Mum's grave would open up and swallow her. Wayne Baker's entire body seemed to radiate with anger. She'd been a fool to stay out in the open in full sight. As she rolled over and tried to get up, Wayne immediately kicked her in the stomach. She clutched at her belly, trying to ease the pain. Somehow, she needed to escape this situation, but in this vulnerable position, lying on the ground, what chance did she stand?

Baker towered above her with his arms folded, saying nothing. What was he waiting for? Why didn't he just finish her off? Rose glanced around, searching frantically for something to use as a weapon. She wondered how deep the wooden cross would be buried. It lurched at a 45-degree angle. Judging by the amount the cross moved when she knocked into it, it should be easy enough to pull it out of the ground, especially after all that rain. But if she made her move too slowly, Baker might grab the cross before she did and use it against her. It would be a huge risk, but she didn't have any other choice.

It started to rain again, the cold droplets stinging her face. Baker stood slap bang in the middle of her mother's grave. Rose hated him for being so disrespectful. Part of her wanted to protect her mother and her memory. If Mum were really here, what would she say? She'd tell

Rose she could do it. She'd tell her she could do anything she put her mind to, and it didn't matter who she was or where she came from. She'd tell her to believe in herself. Rose wished she'd listened to her mother more when she was still alive.

Across the graveyard, a dog barked. As Baker twisted round to look, Rose saw her chance. She grabbed the wooden cross with both hands, pulling it towards her to lever it out of the ground. Gripping it with every last bit of her strength, she whacked it hard across Baker's shins.

Baker yelled. Rose saw the pain in his face, but she hadn't hit him forcefully enough. He lurched forward quickly and grabbed hold of her before she could run.

Frantically, she tried to twist her arm free, but he grabbed the other arm too, pinning both arms to her sides. She kicked him hard in the shin, hoping she'd picked the spot already damaged by the cross. Baker stumbled forwards, ploughing into her. Rose kicked him again, and he fell to the ground, taking her with him.

As Rose tried to catch her breath, Baker rolled over on top of her, pinning her down. He'd lost his grip on her left arm, and suddenly he let go of her right arm too. Rose wriggled both arms out from underneath him, but his hands encircled her neck, so she struggled to breathe. She punched his back feebly. A vision of Jack entered her head. He was with Ash. Jack wouldn't be safe with him. She couldn't die here, not when her son needed her. With a huge effort, she stretched out her right arm. Her fingers touched the smooth glass side of the jam jar. She needed to get closer. With her other hand, she found Baker's ear and twisted it hard.

Baker let go of her neck for a second. She almost forgot to breathe as she stretched to reach the glass jar. She just managed to grab hold of it as Baker's hands encircled her neck once more. She thought of her mother and of Jack as she smashed the jar onto the back of Baker's head, shutting her eyes at the last moment to avoid any flying pieces of glass.

Baker fell forwards onto her, releasing her neck. With a massive effort, she pushed him to one side, wriggling out from underneath his heavy weight.

Rose fought for breath. The agonising pain in her neck almost made her faint. She coughed and spluttered, trying to get air into her lungs.

Next to her, Baker groaned. He rolled onto his side and tried to get up. No way would Rose be able to outrun him now, not with the state of both of them. Baker wasn't in a good way, but Rose still fought for breath. Quickly, she scooped up the broken base of the jam jar. Its jagged shards provided her last hope. As Baker started to get to his feet, she lurched forward, plunging the broken glass into the side of his neck.

Her hand dripped with blood as she pulled it away. She flinched at the gash on her palm, which stung with pain. Was the blood hers or Wayne Baker's? A small red puddle collected on the ground next to Baker. Rose stared at it in a daze. What had she done?

A shout from across the graveyard brought her to her senses. Two men ran towards them. They would call an ambulance for Baker. Rose needed to get out of here before the men reached her. She turned and ran for the gate. No matter that it made her seem guilty. She had to find Jack before anything happened to him.

Chapter 31

DI Waterford drove towards Hale Hill Stores. He'd asked Uniform a few days ago to notify him if they got any calls from the shop or from Rose Marsden. He was worried about her. She'd got involved up to her neck with the Wolfpack gang and didn't even realise how much danger that put her in. They got a call out to the shop where Rose worked from an Alfie Cooper. That name rang a bell from somewhere, but Paul didn't remember exactly where. Apparently, Rose had been attacked by Wayne Baker, then ran off with Baker in pursuit.

He parked his car on a double yellow line and rushed into the shop. Two uniformed officers were talking to a grey-haired man.

"Alfie Cooper?"

"Who's asking?" He looked suspicious.

"Detective Inspector Paul Waterford." Paul showed his ID. "What happened? Where's Rose Marsden? And where is Wayne Baker?"

"I don't know." Cooper looked worried sick. "Rose ran out about twenty minutes ago. Baker followed her. I tried to stop him."

Paul assumed from the bruise forming on Alfie's cheek that he'd been in a fight with Baker. That was brave of him. Stupid, but brave.

"Did you see which direction they went in?"

"They headed that way." Alfie pointed to his right. "But they might have gone anywhere after that."

Paul frowned. Things didn't look good for Mrs Marsden. She'd be no match for Baker if he caught her. The direction Alfie indicated would take her to Eastbury Park, and then on towards Brackford.

"Would she have gone home?"

"I already checked," Alfie said. "She's not answering her door."

Paul's phone rang. He excused himself and stepped outside the shop to answer it.

"Kevin, what's up?" Kevin Farrier had better be calling him with something important. If Baker was on Rose Marsden's tail, she was running out of time. It might be too late already.

"We got a call from Brackford cemetery, guv. Wayne Baker has been attacked. He's badly injured and is on his way to hospital. Witnesses say a woman ran away from the scene. It sounds like Rose Marsden."

"Are the witnesses still at the cemetery?"

"I think so, guv."

"Meet me there," Paul said.

Paul excused himself and drove towards Brackford cemetery. How in the hell did Rose Marsden manage to injure a violent brute like Wayne Baker? She'd been very lucky, if it was her. She might just as easily be lying dead in Eastbury Park by now. Perhaps these witnesses were mistaken. But they would still need to question her about the attack on Baker, even though Paul assumed it would have been self-defence. Did she panic and run when she'd seen the extent of Baker's injuries? She wouldn't be the first person to react like that.

He left his car in the adjoining car park and walked into the cemetery, spotting the crime scene instantly. Yellow police tape surrounded the area, and the white plastic-suited scene of crime officer crouched next to one of the graves. A uniformed officer stood to one side, talking to two men. Paul hoped they might be the witnesses.

Paul walked straight over to the men. "DI Waterford," he said, producing his ID. He turned to the officer. "Are these our witnesses?"

"Yes, guv." The officer introduced them. They were father and son.

"Can you tell me what happened, please?" he asked the men.

"We've just been through all that with this officer here," the father said.

"Sorry, but I need you to go through it again."

"The man was already lying on the ground when we came in. We ran over to help. He was bleeding heavily. I put pressure on the wound and we called an ambulance. There wasn't much else we could do."

"You did the right thing," Paul reassured him. "What about the woman?"

"She ran off before we got here," the son said. "She seemed to be in a real hurry."

"Will he die?" the father asked.

"I'm sure the doctors will try their best." It would be no great loss to society if Wayne Baker didn't make it, but Paul knew better than to say that. "Can you describe the woman?"

"We didn't see her up close. Maybe in her forties, long brown hair."

"Shoulder-length," the father interrupted.

"Yes, shoulder-length brown hair, wearing a red top."

The description fitted Rose Marsden, along with plenty of other women, too. "Thank you," Paul said. They needed to find Ashley Walker. But most of all, they needed to find Rose Marsden before Walker did.

Paul went over to speak to the scene of crime officer Erica as Kevin approached from the other end of the cemetery. He'd taken his time to get here.

"Good to see you, Erica. Any observations so far?"

Erica looked up from her crouched position. "Plenty of blood," she said. "The victim will be lucky to survive this."

Paul noticed there was no headstone on the grave. "We need to find out whose grave this is."

Erica picked up a plastic evidence bag containing a wooden cross. "Iris Brown. Buried last month, hence no proper headstone yet."

"Who's Iris Brown?" Paul asked.

Kevin Farrier joined them. "Iris Brown is Rose Marsden's mother."

Paul grimaced. Was it possible that Baker defiled Iris Brown's grave, and Mrs Marsden lost her temper? He hoped not. He didn't want Rose Marsden up on a murder charge, and certainly not for the sake of a scumbag like Baker.

"We need to find Ashley Walker," Paul said. "Let's start with his house in case he's returned there. Leave your car here and come with me." Farrier took so long to get here from the station, Paul wondered if he had detoured somewhere else on the way. It wouldn't be the first time a DC went on a private errand in the middle of the work day. Paul would deal with that later, but right now, time was critical.

"I'll knock on the door. You go round the back," Paul said when they arrived at Ashley Walker's semi-detached, which he shared with his brother.

They were still sitting in the car making a plan when a silver BMW pulled out of the driveway.

Kevin got a good view of the driver. "That's him," he shouted excitedly.

Paul started the engine and did a rapid U-turn in the road, gunning the car up to speed in pursuit of the BMW.

"Are you sure we've got Ashley this time, not his brother?"

"Yes, guv, it's him all right. I had a few run-ins with him when I was still in uniform. It's definitely him."

Paul regretted not sending Kevin Farrier to Walker's house with Barry this morning. Maybe then, Barry wouldn't have brought in the wrong man.

The BMW cruised along two cars ahead of them. Paul held back, unsure if Ashley had seen them. If not, it would be useful to find out where he was headed.

"Do you think he's seen us, guv?" Kevin read his mind.

"We'll soon find out, but I'm trying to stay well back in case he hasn't." Paul cornered smoothly, dropping down the gears before accelerating out of the turn. Ash was already exceeding the speed limit, giving them plenty of cause to stop him, but in a built-up area like this, Paul didn't want to pressurise him into causing an accident.

"Should we call for backup?"

Paul scowled. "Not yet." The last thing he wanted was to spook Ashley into doing something stupid by setting a string of squad cars on his tail with sirens blaring and blue lights flashing. In any case, when they caught him, there would be two of them and only one of him. They shouldn't need any help.

The BMW turned into a side road. Paul followed. There didn't seem any point in hanging back now. It would soon become obvious they were following. He knew this road—a popular shortcut that would take them onto the main route into Brackford.

"Where did you go on the way to the cemetery?" Paul remained certain that Kevin didn't drive directly there.

"Nowhere," Kevin replied a little too quickly.

Ashley didn't appear to have noticed them yet. Paul realised he soon would, when they made another turn. "Then why did it take you so long to get there?"

"The traffic was bad," Kevin muttered.

Paul glanced over at him. The way he fiddled nervously with his seat belt, no way was he telling the truth.

With no other traffic in sight, the safest thing to do would be to make Ash stop his car before he realised they were following. Paul pulled out, intending to overtake.

Immediately, the BMW swerved into the middle of the road, making it impossible to pass, and speeded up.

"I guess he's seen us, guv," Kevin stated the obvious.

They were driving much too fast for a residential area. If something came the other way, or a pedestrian ran into the road, there would be an accident. Paul slowed down, increasing the distance between them, hoping to take the pressure off and make Ash slow down too. He was confident enough of catching up with the BMW if necessary. Ashley might be driving a slightly more powerful car, but this road took a lot of skill to drive at speed, and Paul could make up ground by negotiating the corners faster.

"You're getting left behind."

"I'm trying not to cause an accident," Paul snapped.

Up ahead, the BMW moved back into the inside lane and took the left-handed bend much too fast, causing the car to drift across the white line in the centre of the road.

"Get onto Control. If they've got any patrol cars in the area, get them to set up a roadblock where this road comes out onto the Brackford road. Fast as you can." Paul wished he'd done that earlier, but the situation had been under control then. Now he worried that Ashley's erratic driving might cause an accident. However much he wanted to apprehend him, the public's safety came first.

Kevin put his mobile onto speakerphone, enabling Paul to join in the conversation. Two patrol cars waited nearby. With a bit of luck, they'd have Ash Walker in custody soon.

"Do you think Baker will be ok?" Kevin asked.

"He'll probably live." As far as Paul was concerned, he'd got what he deserved. "As soon as we've arrested Walker, we'll head over to the hospital and check on Baker. He's probably in surgery now, so it's likely to be ages before we can interview him."

The junction with the Brackford road would be coming up at any moment. Paul steadied the car. In front of them, the BMW still motored along at breakneck speed, but if Walker slammed his brakes on suddenly for a roadblock, Paul wanted to be ready for it. The screech of brakes alerted him to a problem before he rounded the final bend. Up ahead, a patrol car parked halfway across the road signalled a roadblock. The BMW skidded to a halt. Instantly, the car accelerated into reverse, performing a speedy three-point turn.

The patrol car set off in pursuit. Paul swerved across the road, trying to take up enough room to block any chance of Ashley exiting.

"We've got him, guv," Kevin said. "He's trapped at both ends now. There's no way out."

Paul ignored his overwhelming urge to tell Kevin to shut up. There was always a way out. He needed to ensure that Ashley Walker didn't take it.

Chapter 32

The BMW slalomed across the road, with Paul trying to anticipate each move and block it. If Ashley attempted to get past, he would hit him. Paul braced himself, anticipating a bump at the least, if not worse. Ash displayed no sign of slowing down. He was too close now for any chance of him stopping. Was he playing chicken with him? The BMW accelerated straight at him.

"Bloody nutter," Paul shouted as he swerved off to the side, pumping the brakes to slow down without skidding.

The BMW mounted the grass verge at the side of the road, crashing through a white wooden picket fence in the front garden of the corner house. The car smashed straight out the other side, and across the lawn, leaving a trail of splintered white wood in its wake before turning the corner into another side road.

The patrol car followed. Paul turned around. This housing estate was a maze of roads. He may be able to cut him off further down.

"Are you ok?" Paul asked. For once, Kevin hadn't said a word. His face was ghostly white.

Kevin let out a low whistle. "Thought I was a goner there," he said.

Paul took the next corner at speed, keeping a sharp eye out for any sign of other road users. If he remembered correctly, this road ran parallel to the one Ashley Walker just took. He thrust his foot down hard on the accelerator. It annoyed him to lose so much valuable time turning the car around. He would find it difficult to catch up now.

"Kevin, get onto Control, quickly. Get Walker's current position." Paul hoped the patrol car would be updating the police control centre as they drove.

Paul wondered if Walker was familiar with this estate. Even though Paul worked in this area as a police constable, he didn't trust his memory. There were so many side roads, most of them interconnected, but a few with dead ends. They might end up driving in circles all day. With relief, he noted his petrol tank was over half-full.

"There he is, guv." Kevin waved his hands excitedly, pointing in front of them. "He's heading back to the main road."

Paul took a sharp left. If he sped up, he might be able to cut him off. "See if Uniform can get there first. If they can get the stinger in front of the car, that will stop him." The stinger was a spike strip that they fired in front of a car to puncture its tyres. It was the safest way to stop a car. In one respect, Paul didn't like high-speed chases, especially over a long distance. It vastly ramped up the risk of civilians being hurt. Aside from that, he loved them. Nothing else gave the same huge adrenaline rush, but the worry of mowing down an innocent child often outweighed that.

They almost reached the next junction when they saw the silver BMW speeding past on the road up ahead. "Damn, we just missed him," Paul said.

A patrol car followed close behind Walker's car.

"I reckon they're going about eighty," Kevin said.

"In a thirty mph limit." Paul's worry that there would be an accident rocketed skywards.

Paul turned left, following the BMW and the patrol car at a safe distance. Up ahead, he caught a glimpse of another patrol car parked on the kerb. If they deployed the stinger, Ashley Walker would soon be in custody. He steadied his speed, not wanting to get caught up in the carnage when the Beamer hit the stinger.

The BMW accelerated, its powerful engine producing an impressive spurt of speed. The patrol car behind it also accelerated. They were way too close. They must not be expecting the stinger to be deployed. Paul didn't have a police radio in his car. Perhaps they were in communication with the other patrol and knew that there would be no stinger.

A moment later, a flash of silver shot out into the road ahead. The patrol car decelerated rapidly, grinding to a halt. The BMW flew up the road in front of them.

"Sod it," Paul said. "They shot the stinger out too late, got the patrol car instead." He drove his car up on the footway, manoeuvring around the stinger and the grounded patrol car, which sat sideways across the road. Immediately, Paul floored the accelerator. The car responded with a spurt of speed. Paul's car would do zero to sixty in less than five seconds, but that might not be enough. Ashley Walker's BMW was one of the latest M series. Zero to sixty in three or four seconds, if Paul remembered correctly. Walker's car was rapidly disappearing into the distance in a streak of silver. If they lost the BMW before it reached the main road, it would be much harder to find it again. Paul reassured himself he was a highly trained, advanced driver, and Ashley Walker just an amateur. He might be able to catch him before he vanished completely.

"We're gaining on him, guv. Put your foot down."

"What the hell do you think I'm doing?" Paul dropped the car down to third gear on the turn, using the lower gear to gun it up to speed again. They were making up ground.

"Watch out for those kids up ahead," Kevin said.

Paul had already spotted them. Two teenagers on bikes started to cross the road. His heart leapt into his mouth. The BMW wasn't slowing down. Surely, Walker didn't intend to plough into those kids?

At the last moment, the BMW swerved up onto the footway, avoiding the two children by a whisker. Paul breathed a huge sigh of relief. He kept going. Two seconds later, the children had run to the other side of the road, giving him plenty of room to speed past safely. He glanced sideways at them as he passed. They looked ok. No need to stop and check them.

He was still gaining ground on the BMW. Swerving to mount the footway slowed Walker down enough for them to nearly catch him up. The BMW steadied for the junction. Paul was willing to bet he would still take the corner at a fair speed. He took the chance to catch up with him. Somehow, he needed to stop him before he caused an accident. Deftly, he manoeuvred his car into position, then accelerated a touch, catching the BMWs bumper on the outside corner.

The BMW span off the road as Paul slammed his brakes on. Ashley had lost control of the spin. The car ploughed into a thick conifer hedge, coming to a stop with a sudden jolt.

"Get out, quick. Stop him before he gets away," Paul shouted to Kevin.

Kevin raced towards the driver's door as it opened. Paul got out of the car and ran towards the BMW.

"Stay where you are," Kevin shouted. He pulled the door open fully, grabbing Ashley's arm. "Now, get out of the vehicle." He twisted Ashley's arm behind his back, snapping on handcuffs. "Ashley Walker, you're under arrest."

As Kevin read him his rights, Paul phoned for a patrol car to come and pick up Ashley. It was a great relief to get both him and Wayne Baker safely in custody, but they still needed to find Rose Marsden. He hoped for her sake that she'd injured Baker in self-defence. There surely couldn't be any other reason, but he needed to remain open-minded. As soon as the patrol car showed up for Ashley, they would go to the hospital to check on Baker, then they would search for Mrs Marsden.

Chapter 33

Rose soon found the footpath at the back of the cemetery and started to run. She didn't have time to dawdle, despite the path being stony and narrow. The police had been planning to arrest Ash at his house early this morning, so if Ash collected Jack from the station this afternoon, either the police raid must have failed, or they had to let him go. She cursed her stupid phone battery for running out at the worst time possible. Now she wished she'd called the police earlier because the warehouse was a long shot. Ash might have taken Jack anywhere. But the warehouse was the only place she knew of that was connected to Ash. The property belonged to his cousin, so even if he and Jack weren't there, she may find someone who could tell her where to find Ash.

The footpath ran along the back of a row of houses for a stretch. As she ran, the pounding of her footsteps alerted a dog in one of the gardens on the other side of the fence. Without warning, it ran towards the fence, barking ferociously, distracting Rose. Suddenly, her leg collapsed underneath her. She let out a small scream as the pain shot through her ankle. For a moment, she stood on one leg, trying to catch her breath. She'd twisted her ankle. The large stone she'd trodden on lay guiltily in the middle of the path.

Rose sat on the ground, rubbing her ankle. Hopefully, it would be ok in a couple of minutes. On the other side of the fence, the dog continued to bark at her. Even when she shouted at it to shut up, the damn dog wouldn't stop. She wanted to cry. Jack was depending on her, but instead of being sensible and reporting everything to the police, she'd run off all gung-ho on a wild goose chase. And now she was stuck in the middle of nowhere, unable to walk, with a dead phone battery.

She continued to rub her ankle. It felt a little better. She reminded herself it would have been risky to wait for the police. Wayne Baker had looked seriously injured. What if he bled to death? If she got arrested for his murder, the police would prioritise that. They wouldn't put any effort into looking for a nineteen-year-old man, missing for less than an hour. She needed to find Jack herself. Rose shuddered as she remembered Wayne threatening earlier to kill Jack if she didn't cooperate. That must be why Ash went to pick him up. It was too much of a coincidence for him to just show up at the station by chance. If anything happened to Jack, it would be all her fault.

After a few minutes, Rose got to her feet, cautiously testing her weight on her twisted ankle. She decided to risk continuing on. Further along the path lay some broken tree branches, probably lobbed over the fence from one of the houses that backed onto the footpath. She sorted through them, picking out a sturdy branch of a suitable length to use as a walking stick. She set off slowly, using the stick to help take some of the weight off her bad ankle. Hopefully, she didn't have too much further to go.

Jack woke up. Where the hell was he? His hands were stretched uncomfortably above him. He pulled at them, but there seemed to be something tied around his wrists. Yanking harder got him nowhere. His arms ached like crazy and his head throbbed. How did he get here, and where was Ash?

His memory slowly came back to him. Ash picked him up from Brackford station. He was supposed to be going to Mum's, but Ash drove off in the wrong direction, saying he needed to take him somewhere else first. He tried to remember where they'd driven, but his mind drew a blank and, in any case, he wasn't familiar enough with the area to recognise where he'd been. The only thing he recalled was Ash promising to let him drive his BMW one day soon, even though Jack hadn't even taken his driving test yet.

He shouted out Ash's name, hoping his friend would hear him and untie his arms. This must be some sort of practical joke, but he didn't find it funny.

This room seemed vaguely familiar, but he couldn't place it. He'd tried to shout, but they'd taped up his mouth, so nothing more than a muffled squeak came out. He guessed he would just have to wait until Ash returned. He racked his brain, unable to recall what he might have done to upset Ash, what he might have done to deserve this. He'd give Ash a real piece of his mind when he came back, after he'd untied him. This was no way to treat a mate.

Chapter 34

Wayne Baker was still in surgery when Paul and Kevin arrived at the hospital. Paul asked to speak to one of the doctors. He needed to get some idea of the extent of Baker's injuries and whether he would survive.

While they waited in the corridor, a nurse approached them.

"Hey there, I didn't expect you back so soon." The nurse smiled.

Paul realised she was talking to Kevin. Everything started to make sense. Was this where he'd been earlier? He glared at Kevin, who appeared decidedly uncomfortable.

"Your dad's doing fine," the nurse said. "We'll keep him in overnight, but he should be able to go home in the morning."

"Thank you," Kevin mumbled as the nurse rushed off.

"What was that about?" Paul asked.

"Sorry, guv. My dad was in an accident at work. Got concussed."

"So you bunked off to see him without telling anyone." Paul would probably do the same in that situation.

Kevin nodded. He looked worried.

Paul sighed. "You should have told me. I would have let you go. Of course I would. But what if anything happened, and we didn't know where you were?" Paul was relieved that Kevin hadn't been up to anything dodgy. He just wished he'd said something instead of going off on his own.

"Sorry, guv."

"Do you need to spend some time with your dad now?"

"No, guv. The nurse says he's ok. I can come back after work," Kevin said.

"I'll make sure you finish on time."

"Is one of you DI Waterford?" a voice behind them asked.

Paul turned around quickly. "Yes, that's me."

"Wayne Baker is just finishing up in theatre. It was touch and go for a while, but he's going to be all right."

"Thank you," Paul said. He would make sure an officer guarded him when he woke up. It didn't sound like Baker would be escaping anytime soon, but he didn't want to take any chances.

Chapter 35

Rose gazed at the giant shadow of the warehouse looming above the houses in front of her. The pain in her ankle started to ease, though she wasn't sure she'd be able to run far if she needed to. She still relied on the stick to help her walk. If she kept as much pressure as possible off her ankle now, it might hold up in an emergency.

She tried to work out if it would be quicker to turn right or left to get behind the houses to the warehouse. The distance looked shorter to the right. While she walked, she tried to make a plan, but she didn't even know yet if she'd be able to get inside the warehouse, or if she would find Jack there.

The houses alongside the footpath blocked out the view of the warehouse as she got closer, giving her nothing to navigate by. Usually, her sense of direction sucked, but she seemed to be going the right way. She found an alleyway that looked like it would cut through to the back of the houses and started walking down it.

When she reached the other end, she saw no sign of the warehouse, which she'd expected to be in front of her. The river gushed angrily up ahead. If she stayed near the river edge, she was sure to find the warehouse. As she approached the swirling water, she looked around. A great green monstrosity of a building stood next to the riverbank. However did she miss it? There must have been a bend in the road somewhere, so she'd walked too far and gone past it. Cautiously, she moved towards the warehouse, trying to remain inconspicuous and blend into the trees on the footway. Ahead of her, the statue of Agatha Lee stood tall, reassuring her she had found the right place. She scanned the building as she neared it. Where would be the easiest place to get in? A large padlock secured the main door, but there might be a side entrance with easier access.

Rose pushed her way through some bushes towards the back of the building, searching for another way in. She wished now that she'd told

Jack everything, although he never would have believed her about Darren and Ash. Either way, it meant he would now have no idea how dangerous Ash might be. Probably Darren too. She hoped for Tanya's sake that Darren wasn't wrapped up in this mess.

The path ran out as she turned the corner, and overgrown brambles at the back of the building blocked any way through. Rose retraced her steps, hoping to find a door on the other side of the building.

She stopped for a minute, leaning against the wall to rest her leg. The stick definitely helped, but her ankle still pained her.

On the far side of the warehouse, the path seemed well-trodden. To Rose's relief, it led to another door. A padlock secured this door too, but nothing like the big, heavy-duty one on the front entrance. This one seemed to be of cheap quality, with a long, thin shank.

Rose poked the end of her walking stick through the padlock shank, which thankfully proved just large enough to accommodate the stick. She used the long stick as a lever to put pressure on the padlock, leaning all her weight on the other end of the stick. The wood creaked ominously and Rose hoped her precious walking stick wouldn't break. Suddenly, the padlock snapped open and Rose fell forward as the stick came loose. She put her hands against the door to steady herself. As quickly as possible, she pulled off the padlock, throwing it into the bushes so no one would be tempted to snap it on again.

She picked up her stick and opened the door quietly, pausing in the doorway to listen for any signs of life inside. The building sounded empty. She wanted to shout out for Jack but didn't dare in case Ash was still in here. The building must surely be empty, since the door was padlocked from the outside, but if the last few weeks taught Rose anything, it was caution.

The walking stick made too much noise on the floor, echoing in the big empty building. She would have to do without it. She tucked it under her arm and walked as silently as possible, ignoring the pain in her ankle.

The ground floor consisted mainly of a big warehouse space, empty save for a couple of forklift trucks. Rose took the stairs up to the mezzanine floor, which seemed to be office space.

Upstairs comprised four offices. She tried each door in turn but found no sign of any people, no sign of Jack. Despondent, she sat down in the last office, sinking into the comfortable office chair, relieved at being able to take the weight off her foot for a minute. She wondered about using the phone to call DI Waterford but didn't have his number. Perhaps she should dial 999, report Jack as an abduction to the police. They would have to do something then, wouldn't they?

She swung around in the chair towards the window behind her. She'd been so sure she would find Jack here. Instead, she'd broken into an empty building like a common criminal, and she was still worried sick about Jack.

She realised why the desk was arranged so the occupier of the office would sit with their back to the window. The view didn't inspire. The window overlooked another similar warehouse. Suddenly, a light flashed through her brain. There were two warehouses. She'd got the wrong building. Immediately, she jumped up, grabbed her stick, and hurried down the stairs.

The other warehouse was set further back from the road and was smaller. It would have been easy to overlook it, approaching as she did from the other direction. Rose searched for a side door, finding one quickly. Someone had already smashed the lock on the door. Now Rose regretted dashing over here in such a hurry. She should have used the phone in the other warehouse to call the police. What if anyone was inside this second warehouse? She scouted around the building for signs of any vehicles parked outside but saw nothing close by. She didn't have time to wait and get help. Besides, if the police found her now, she'd be stuck with answering their questions about Wayne Baker for hours, if not longer. Then she'd have no control over whether anyone searched for Jack, or whether he'd be shoved to the bottom of the heap as a low priority. She opened the door.

Rose paused to listen for any signs of life before proceeding. This building differed from the one next door. Large stacks of boxes filled the warehouse floor, the packaging giving no indication of the contents. Rose noted with relief that the boxes weren't big enough to hide a body inside.

Suddenly, a sound on the upper floor made her jump. She ducked down behind a pile of boxes and waited. If there was anyone up there, she didn't want to confront them. She held her breath. The sound of male voices drifted down the stairs. She strained to try to make out some words. The voices were too unclear, but the sound of footsteps on the concrete floor above her told her the speakers were moving towards the stairs.

"We need to get rid of him," the first voice said.

Rose's blood froze. Was Jack somewhere upstairs? She fought to stop herself from running out to confront the men. She concentrated on her breathing, trying to calm herself. If they were leaving, she might avoid a confrontation and go upstairs to search for Jack.

"I parked the car five minutes down the road," a new voice said. "If we walk there separately, we won't draw any attention to ourselves. We'll be miles away by the time anyone notices."

Rose shrunk back behind the boxes as they came down the stairs.

"I'll go first," the first voice spoke. "You do the business, then follow me in five minutes."

"You'd better not go without me." The voice sounded threatening.

What did the man mean when he said *do the business*? He'd already said something about *getting rid of him*. Rose shuddered. Was Jack upstairs? If that second man went back upstairs, she was going to follow. And if he planned to kill her Jack, she couldn't just sit here and do nothing. He'd have to kill her first. Perhaps she would persuade him to let Jack go and keep her instead. She'd do anything to keep her son alive.

A rustling noise close to Rose startled her. She'd been so focused on watching the stairs, she didn't notice the man approaching. She clutched at her stick, unsure what she would do if he found her here. Her only chance might be to poke the stick into one of his vulnerable spots. She would have to be quick before he got the chance to grab it from her. Perhaps it wouldn't come to that. Perhaps he would ignore his friend's instructions to get rid of the person upstairs and leave the building instead.

Suddenly, he turned around and ran towards the door, slamming it behind him as he left. Rose breathed a sigh of relief. He'd left so quickly he wouldn't be back. She eased herself up, shaking the stiffness out of her legs. Her ankle felt a little less painful now. She picked up her walking stick and slid out of her hiding place.

Immediately, a flash of orange flame stopped her in her tracks. The warehouse was on fire, and all those cardboard boxes would go up like a blazing inferno in no time. She searched frantically for a fire extinguisher, desperate to put out the blaze before it got any bigger, but she found nothing. She needed to get upstairs fast and find Jack.

Rose raced up the stairs two at a time, ignoring her throbbing ankle. The first office she checked was empty. She kept going, the flickering flames from downstairs reflecting on the white painted doors.

She opened the door to the second office. "Jack," she screamed. He was standing against the wall, his arms tied up above him to a beam, his head hanging down with exhaustion.

Immediately, he jerked his head up. His eyes flashed surprise, and he said something, the word muffled by the tape over his mouth. She ripped it off.

"Mum! What's going on?" Jack asked.

Rose pulled open all the drawers in the office, looking for something to cut him down. She found a pair of scissors, stood on a chair, and used the scissors to gnaw at the thin rope binding Jack's hands.

"Don't worry." She needed to reassure him. That's what mothers did, and she'd suddenly gone into full maternal mode, protecting her offspring from anything bad. Except that, with each second that passed, the fire downstairs would be taking more of a hold. They needed to get out of the building fast.

"Of course I'm worried," Jack said. "What are you doing here?"

Rose ignored the question. "Where's Ash?" Had he been the one to order setting the fire?

"I don't know." Jack's face looked strained. "Ash picked me up from the station, but then he brought me here and two men tied me up."

It seemed like forever before the scissors finally broke through the rope. Jack shook his arms, trying to restore his circulation.

"We need to get out," Rose said. "The building's on fire."

Chapter 36

Rose ran with Jack towards the fire door on the first floor. It was locked. "We have to go downstairs," Rose said. "We're too high up to jump out the window." The high ceiling of the warehouse below made this upstairs floor way higher than a normal first floor would be.

"We should phone the fire brigade."

"There's no time," Rose said, remembering the dead battery on her phone. "Do you have your phone?"

"No, they took it."

Rose already assumed they would have. There may be phones in the offices, but they couldn't risk being trapped. They raced down the stairs.

The door near the bottom of the stairs, the one Rose had entered through, was locked. The blaze had already taken hold on the warehouse floor. The heat from the fire scorched her face, making her turn away.

"There's a window." Jack pointed at a small window on the far side of the warehouse. "If we run, we can get past the fire."

He grabbed Rose's hand, pulling her along before she got a chance to protest. If the window wouldn't open, they'd be trapped. They were trapped anyway. Rose couldn't see any other way out.

Jack yanked at the handle on the window. It didn't move. He tugged at it uselessly.

Rose handed him her stick. "Break the glass." There would be just enough room for them to climb out. She stood back while Jack smashed the glass from its frame.

Jack put his head out the window. "There's a ledge at ground level, then it slopes down to the river. We'll need to creep along the ledge carefully or we'll fall in the river." He turned back to Rose. "You go first, Mum. I'll help you out."

The fire crept closer to them, its heat intensifying, making it impossible now to go back the way they came. Jack helped lift Rose up and lowered her, feet first, out the window. She felt for the ledge beneath her feet, clinging onto Jack's arms. The rush of water from the river below scared her. She hated swimming.

A cold breeze drifted up from the river, in sharp contrast to the searing heat inside the warehouse. Rose moved along the ledge to give Jack room to get out of the building. She pressed her body against the wall, edging sideways.

Jack came out the window feet first. A few seconds later, he stood on the ledge beside her. "It's ok, Mum. Take your time."

"We need to get away, in case they come back."

"They'd be mad to come back now. Someone will call the fire brigade. The area will be teeming with people soon."

Rose glanced down at the river and gulped. Jack was right. She wasn't thinking straight. She just wanted to get somewhere safe after her ordeal so far this afternoon. And she wanted to get Jack thoroughly checked out.

Rose looked over at Jack. He wasn't moving. She shouted at him. "Are you ok?"

"I'm fine. My arms have gone numb. Keep going. I'll catch you up."

Rose concentrated on stepping sideways as quickly as she could. A sudden movement made her jump, and she heard Jack shout. Rose looked along the ledge, fighting the dizziness that threatened to overwhelm her. Jack must have lost his footing and slipped. He was skidding down the muddy bank on his side, towards the water.

Chapter 37

Rose gasped, watching helplessly as Jack slid rapidly down the slippery riverbank. She tried to stay calm as he twisted awkwardly before splashing noisily into the water at an odd angle. Jack was a strong swimmer. He'd be ok. She started counting, waiting for him to surface. One, two, three... Where was he? Four, five... He should have come up for air by now. Six... It was taking too long. Why hadn't he come to the surface? What if he hit his head as he fell into the water?

Rose crouched down, lowering herself carefully onto the bank. It was dangerously muddy from the recent rain, but it sloped less steeply here than the area further along where Jack fell. She slid down the bank on her bottom, using her hands and feet to try to control the speed. She'd lost count of how many seconds Jack had been under. Taking a deep breath, she slipped into the icy water.

Ducking under the water, Rose forced herself to open her eyes. Jack was drifting slowly towards her. She grabbed his arm and broke the surface of the water, pulling him up with her. He seemed to be stuck on something. She tugged harder, but his face remained underwater. Plucking up all her courage, she duck dived under the water again. A thick knotted bundle of river weed was tangled firmly around one of his trainers. Quickly, she pulled off his shoe, then kicked herself back up to the surface. Jack floated up with her and she immediately cupped her hand under his chin to keep his head above water.

Rose saw some people at the end of the building and screamed at them for help. She would never lift Jack onto the bank by herself. A minute later, a couple of firefighters extended a ladder down the bank. One of the firefighters climbed down to them.

"It's ok," he reassured Rose. "I've got him." He pulled Jack out onto the bank, then extended a hand to Rose.

"Is he breathing?" Rose ignored the hand and grabbed the bottom rung of the ladder instead, heaving herself out of the water. "Help him, please."

The firefighter turned Jack onto his side. Immediately, Jack coughed several times. Rose's whole being flooded with relief. She started to shiver, not sure how much it was from the cold and how much from fear.

The firefighter turned to her. "Can you climb up the ladder?" he asked. "Then my colleague can come down and help me with the young man."

"He's my son." Rose hauled herself up onto the ladder. "His name's Jack."

As she neared the top of the ladder, the second firefighter grabbed her arms and pulled her up. "Can you manage the rest of the way? It's only a few more feet to the end of the building."

Rose nodded. She wanted to stay and make sure Jack was all right, but she needed to get out of the way to allow the firefighters to get him out quickly.

As she reached the end of the building, another firefighter met her, along with two paramedics. She insisted on waiting until they brought Jack out. They strapped him onto the ladder, using it as a stretcher.

"He may have hit his head," a cheerful sounding paramedic said. "Was he unconscious for long?"

"He went underwater for a few seconds," Rose said. How long was it really? Perhaps more than a few seconds. "Will he be all right?"

"Stop fussing, Mum."

Rose was overjoyed to hear Jack's voice.

"Let's get you both to hospital and warm you up."

As the paramedic closed the ambulance doors, Rose noticed the massive plumes of black smoke rising skywards. Her nose was too bunged up from being in the water to smell anything, but she saw the fire clearly now. They'd had a lucky escape.

Chapter 38

Rose opened another bottle of wine and topped up everyone's glasses. "I'd like to propose a toast to my wonderful son, Jack." She thrust her glass forwards, clinking it against each of her guests' glasses, one by one.

"Mum." Jack groaned with embarrassment.

"I'm just so glad you're still in one piece, darling." A couple of days ago, she might so easily have lost him. She smiled, a big beaming smile. "To Jack," she said, clinking on the last of the glasses. She felt mildly tipsy now, but it was so wonderful to have her son safe, and great to have her friends here too.

Rose glanced round the table at her guests. Sarah, who took a chance on her, giving her a job when she was unemployable. Alfie, a constant tower of strength, who risked his neck for her more than once. And Dorothy, who provided a shoulder to cry on during some of the worst moments of her life. She wished Tan had shown up, but perhaps she hadn't forgiven her yet for accusing Darren of being involved in the Wolfpack gang. Rose hoped they would make it up soon, because she valued Tanya's friendship, and she was fun to have around. If ever Rose needed some fun, it was now.

"Well, I'd like to propose a toast to Rose." Sarah raised her glass, which was almost empty already. "Without you, I don't suppose Roman's murderer would ever have been caught." Sarah quietly wiped a tear from her eye and forced a smile.

"Yes, you were amazing, Rose," Alfie said. "Even if you had me worried sick about your safety half the time. How did you realise about Wayne Baker?"

Rose smiled. "Call it female intuition." For the sake of her safety, and Jack's, she would never admit to anyone how much she saw in the shop on that first night of her return to Mum's flat when Roman was murdered. The police had collected enough evidence to tie him to the Terry Thompson murder too: some CCTV footage close to Eastbury

Park and a dropped glove with Wayne Baker's DNA on it, as well as gunpowder residue. On top of that, some other local businesses had come forward with evidence of the protection racket.

Rose got up. "We've still got dessert."

"I'm stuffed, Rose," Alfie said. "You've fed me far too well already, but I'll watch the rest of you eat it."

"You'll want some of this," she said.

As she went to the fridge to fetch dessert, Rose noticed the light on her phone flash. She checked it quickly. It showed two missed calls from Tan, but no voicemail. Perhaps she'd called to apologise for not showing up. Rose would go round to her flat tomorrow and try to patch things up with her properly.

"That looks delicious," Alfie said as Rose placed the huge bowl of homemade chocolate mousse on the table.

Rose put a big serving spoon next to it. "It's chocolate raspberry mousse. Help yourself." She'd decorated it with fresh raspberries, and it did look rather good. As she predicted, Alfie dived in first. Her other guests didn't take long to empty the bowl.

"This is yummy," Alfie said.

"You weren't full up after all." Rose laughed. She'd noticed a few times Alfie could always make some room for chocolate.

Her phone rang.

"Aren't you going to answer that?" Sarah asked.

"It's probably Tan. I've already got a couple of missed calls from her. I expect she's phoning to apologise for not showing up."

"She's probably working," Alfie said.

"I'm sure she could have changed her shift if she'd really wanted to come," Rose said. She guessed Tan wasn't that bothered about their friendship after all.

Alfie laughed. "I don't think it works like that, not in her line of business."

"What do you mean? She's in customer services, isn't she?" She only ever seemed to work the night shifts, but Rose assumed that paid better.

"Customer services? I suppose you might call it that. She's a prostitute," Alfie said.

"What makes you say that?" Tan seemed like a nice enough woman. Rose struggled to imagine her selling her body for a living.

"Are you one of her customers, Alfie?" Jack asked, winking at him.

"I can't afford it," Alfie said dryly. "But it's obvious, isn't it? She works nights and goes to work tarted up in high heels and sexy outfits. And that son of hers is up to no good. Wouldn't surprise me if he's pimping her."

"So you're just guessing, then?" Rose said. She would prefer to give Tanya the benefit of the doubt.

"I've met her type before," Alfie said.

Jack started to say something, but Alfie glared at him and he shut up.

Sarah looked at her watch. "I really need to go home," she said. "I've left Maggie Mahoney babysitting the girls. She won't want to stay too late. Thank you for a wonderful evening, Rose." She got up.

"Thank you for coming," Rose said. "And thank you, everybody. I would never have got through the last few weeks without you."

"I'll walk you home," Alfie said to Sarah, gallant as ever.

"I'd better go home too." Dorothy got up from the table.

The flat seemed quiet when they'd all left.

"Do you need a hand with the washing-up?" Jack asked.

"No. You take it easy." Rose still worried about Jack, who wasn't quite back to normal after nearly drowning two days ago.

She shut the kitchen door behind her and started running water into the washing-up bowl. At least there were no leftovers to tidy up, as everyone loved her food. It reminded her of the old days, in Manchester, when she and Philip often invited people round for dinner. Fighting back the pang of nostalgia, she set to work washing the large pile of dirty dishes.

Halfway through, her phone rang again. It was 11:00 p.m. She'd better answer it. It might be urgent.

Tan's name glowed on the caller ID.

"Hello." Rose wasn't quite sober enough to have a sensible conversation with Tan. Immediately, she regretted answering.

"Rose, I need your help." Background noise on the phone distorted Tanya's voice. It sounded like something rustling.

"What's the matter?"

No reply came.

"Tan. Tan, are you there? What's up?" Rose heard more rustling noises on the line.

"Tanya?" Rose tried again. The phone clicked, and the line went dead.

Immediately, Rose dialled Tan's number. No answer. Tanya had seemed distressed. Something was wrong, and she didn't know what to do.

THE END

Before you go, turn the page to find out what happens next...

STONE COLD

Book 2 in The Murder Mile series

The clues to the present lie in the past...

Rose Marsden is struggling with the revelation that her new friend, Tanya, is a prostitute. So, when Tanya goes missing, and her son begs Rose for help, she's reluctant to get involved.

But when a young prostitute's body is dumped at the base of a local statue, and Rose discovers that Tanya was the last person to see the girl alive, she knows she must find Tanya, before somebody else does.

As Rose delves deeper, she gets involved with a protest group campaigning to have the statue removed, hoping it will lead her to her missing friend. Instead, the discovery of an innocent schoolgirl's body in the same place sparks fears of a serial killer.

Tanya is still missing. Is it possible that she's the murderer, or will she become the next victim?

A page-turning mystery-thriller with compelling characters. Stone Cold is the second book in The Murder Mile series, but can be read as a standalone.

Available on Amazon

ROCK BOTTOM

Discover how Rose ends up living in her mother's flat. Rock Bottom is the prequel to The Murder Mile series. It's **FREE** to download when you sign up to my author newsletter.

The locals call it the Murder Mile because of the rising number of murders, but she didn't expect her own mother to be one of the victims.

When Rose Marsden receives the devastating news of her mother's death, she rushes to London to find out what's going on. At first, it looks like a burglary gone wrong.

As she struggles to come to terms with her tragic loss, the shocking revelation that her mother died of a drug overdose rocks her world still further. The police have labelled her mother as a junkie and closed the case, but Rose is certain her mother would never touch drugs. She is desperate to find out the truth and get justice for her mum.

Despite her efforts, Rose is frustrated by lack of proof, and her own safety is put at risk during a frightening encounter with a local gang member. Now, fear of reprisal means the only way to survive is to find evidence to convict the murderer.

The Hale Hill estate is a dangerous place. Will Rose's stubborn persistence turn her into the next victim?

Be the first to find out about new releases, special offers, and other interesting stuff. Download the free book and sign up using this link: https://dl.bookfunnel.com/6vtvzlvamf

Other Books by the Author

If you liked INTO THE RED, you may also like the **Clarke Pettis series**, which is set in and around Brackford and features some of the same characters. Available on Amazon.

Book 1 THE FRAUD
A chance discovery of a fraud turns into a terrifying ordeal. Can Clarke find the courage she needs to unravel the web of lies and escape from an impossible situation?

Book 2 THE COVER-UP
A routine job becomes threatening when Clarke finds a body in the company's research lab. The employees all have their own issues, but which one has been driven to murder?

Book 3 THE PAYBACK
Clarke finds herself in serious danger when a fugitive becomes obsessed with revenge.

About The Author

Christine Pattle writes mystery-thrillers with compelling characters and interesting plots. Her aim is always to write a good page-turning story that readers will love.

When she's not writing, she's busy scaring herself silly, riding big, feisty horses, or walking round the countryside dreaming up exciting new plots.

You can contact Christine at christine@christinepattleauthor

Or visit her Facebook page: christinepattleauthor

Acknowledgments

A HUGE thank you:

To you, the reader. Readers are by far the most important people in an author's world. Of all the millions of books you could have chosen to read, a massive THANK YOU for giving my book a chance. I really hope you enjoyed it. If you can spare a few minutes to leave a review for the book on Amazon, or even a couple of seconds to give it a star rating, I would be very grateful. It helps other readers to discover my books and inspires me to keep on writing.

To my brilliant editor, Emily at Laurence Editing.

To my cover artist, Get Covers.

And, lastly, to all the authors who have ever inspired me. I love reading.

COPYRIGHT

Printed in Great Britain
by Amazon

35786140R00121